WARNED

THE ASTROLOGER'S PROPHECY

MAHTAB NARSIMHAN

WARNED : The Astrologer's Prophecy

EERIE TALES FROM THE EAST : BOOK 1

For more information, go to: www.mahtabnarsimhan.com

Cover Design by PINTADO

Book Design by Mahtab Narsimhan

Published by Stardust Stories

ISBN Print Book: 978-1-7778318-1-3

First Edition: February 2022

For the Fantastic Masterminds
Couldn't have done it without you.

1

The line outside the astrologer's tent snaked through the village fair—long and sinuous. I wondered if he was that good. Not that I believed in any of the rubbish superstitions or fortune- telling that seemed to be the case here.

My phone rang half-heartedly. I grabbed it and pressed talk, afraid I would lose the weak signal if I moved.

"Hey, Lee!" I said. "Miss you, man. How's Delhi?" Lee was my best friend and miles away. I should have been there with him, or he should have been here. I tried to ignore the pang in my gut when I thought of two weeks in this remote village without a friend.

"Miss you too," he said. "Delhi seems weird without you. Where are you again?" His voice crackled and broke. The signal was so terrible I was scared I'd lose him.

"Tolagunj," I said. "Small village up north. My grandfather is some bigshot here with the title of zamindar. Something like a head honcho with lots of land." I swatted a large wasp that buzzed by. My fingers touched the EpiPen in my pocket and my heartbeat slowed. As long as I had it with me at all times, I was okay. No wasp could hurt me.

"What are you planning to do there for two weeks?" Lee asked.

"Probably die of boredom," I said, gazing at the villagers milling around food stalls, the cows and goats wandering by, the amateur game stalls. "I brought boo—" I started to say when someone snatched the phone out of my hand.

I whirled around and there he was—a weirdo in a black kaftan and a fancy turban of colored beads that covered his face. He gripped my arm and dragged me into the tent, despite the grumbling villagers in line.

"How dare you?" I squeaked, my eyes darting around the bare tent. "This is child abuse!"

"I'm an astrologer and I see grave danger in your aura," he said. The beads swayed and tinkled as he spoke. "Leave now or you'll die a horrible death!" Stinking of sweat and sandalwood, he leaned close. "This year the wasps are the worst I've ever seen. Enough of them sting you and you're dead," he hissed.

I stared at him, aghast. "Who told you I'm allergic to wasps? They do nothing to me." Yet he'd spoken the truth. Probably a lucky guess.

"The nearest hospital is fifty kilometers from here," he said in a whisper. "Want to take your chances?" The heat in the tent was stifling.

"Give me my phone," I said, jerking my head toward his hand.

"Will you leave if I do?" asked the astrologer.

"Who are you to tell me what I should do?" I said. "And no. I won't." I shuffled backward out of the tent and bumped into a villager, who grumbled loudly.

The astrologer followed, his black eyes boring into mine from behind the curtain of beads. Barefoot, he stood there and surveyed the line of waiting customers. Sweat pooled at the base of his neck, which he wiped away with a grimy hand and then muttered under his breath, making the complaining villager blanch.

This guy was a weirdo and a bully. He'd probably seen me swat at that wasp when I was talking to Lee and predicted that I feared them to get me to pay him. I'd read somewhere that most fortune-tellers had excellent powers of observation. There was no way I was parting with any money for this fraud, even though he'd made a lucky guess.

"I say this for your own good," said the astrologer. "Why do you want to die young?"

"You're making this up just to scare me," I said, stepping out of reach before he grabbed me again. "You saw me swat that wasp earlier. It's summer so there will be lots of them around. You're a fraud."

"Only one way to find out," he said. "You're in grave danger here, and I have warned you. Your parents will lose their only child."

An electric current jolted through me. *How did he know this stuff?*

"Phone!" I said.

The astrologer slapped it into my hand, muttering under his breath. If he thought I'd react the same way as a villager, he was sadly mistaken.

"I don't believe your predictions," I said. Though it felt like an army of mice were running up and down my spine, I wouldn't let him see that he'd rattled me. It would only make him spout more crap or lucky guesses.

His laugh was chilling. The beads in his headdress clattered together softly. "Then stay, and you'll see that I'm right. Your poor parents." He dismissed me with a wave of his hand and turned to a waiting villager.

I looked around for Mom and Dad. I had to try once

more (and only the billionth time!) to plead with them to let me stay with my friend Lee in Delhi, while they were volunteering as doctors in Rajasthan. This desert state was suffering from serious drought and illnesses among its farmers. They'd already told me Nana was a technophobe and there'd be no Wi-Fi at his place. I was going to be bored out of my mind in Tolagunj. They couldn't expect me to read books for two entire weeks. Unless I died before that. I tried not to think about it as I hurried through the fair, looking for Mom.

I found her talking to a man wearing a white dhoti-kurta and a snow-white turban, with a face like a prune. When I walked over to her, she put an arm around my shoulders. "Avi, this is Mr. Venkat, the head of the panchayat in Tolagunj. The panchayat settles disputes in the village, much like a court in the city," she added when she saw my puzzled expression.

"Um . . . okay," I said, not really interested in anything except that she'd let me go back to Delhi.

"I threw up on him as a kid," Mom continued, laughing. "Mr. Venkat, this is my son, Avijeet."

TMI.

Mr. Venkat gave a hearty laugh, which sounded totally fake. I managed a weak smile.

"I have to talk to you, Mom," I said. "It's urgent."

She gave me the stink eye. "Excuse me," she said to Mr. Venkat. "I'll be right back."

As soon as we were out of eavesdropping range, she shook her head as if she already knew what I was going to say. She was right. "No, Avi, we're not leaving. You will stay here with Nana. It will be a pleasant change of pace for you, and good for him too. He's been very lonely since Nani died."

"So *you* spend time with him," I snapped. "Let me stay with Lee. Please, Mom. This place feels weird—people are lining up outside an astrologer's tent to have their fortunes told!" I refused to tell her about my brief encounter with him.

"The villagers are very superstitious," said Mom. "Don't hold it against them. I know Nana did not want us to come, but I think he needs his family. Besides, we're only staying a week in Rajasthan and the second week we'll all be together. I'll show you my favorite hikes around here. We'll have fun, I promise."

"Mom, any house without Wi-Fi and cell coverage is child abuse," I said. "I can barely get one bar on the phone here."

She laughed. "Sue me. Meet us at the car in twenty."

I wandered through narrow aisles between stalls set up in the village square. It was loud and noisy. Smells of fried food, parched earth, and manure filled the air. So unlike the city, where it would have been the smells of coffee, petrol, and garbage. I missed the white noise of traffic and was already homesick.

Villagers, dressed in bright clothes with the men sporting colorful turbans, called out to me to buy food or play a game. I ignored them all, trying not to feel too sorry for myself. If I really thought about it, I guess I could put this time to good use and finish writing my scary story and read a ton of books.

A plump vendor with a double chin was selling *gulab jamuns*—fried sweets dipped in sugar syrup. A cloud of flies perched on the wire dome covering them, but not a single one had got through the mesh. *Good!*

"I'll have five, please," I said, pulling out a ten-rupee note.

The vendor slipped tongs under the dome, plucked five golden-brown balls and put them into a cone made of dried banana leaves. He handed me the change.

I walked slowly, savoring the rich sweetness in my mouth. A prickle at the back of my neck made me pause. Someone was watching me. I glanced around, but no one seemed to be looking my way. The villagers wandered in and out of stalls, chatting or playing games, while kids whooped and darted around in the late afternoon sunshine. Cows with tinkling bells chewed the cud. Stray dogs scrounged in piles of garbage beside the stalls.

Was the astrologer stalking me? But he was nowhere around.

A shadow between two stalls moved. A young girl was sweeping up the garbage into a handheld pan with a small broom. She was dark-skinned and wore a heavily patched kurta-pajama with a white dupatta draped over her head. Red bangles on her arms clinked softly as she swept, her eyes riveted to the sweets in my hand.

She looked away when she saw that I'd noticed her. She was so thin her cheekbones stood out like twin peaks on either side of her nose. The mouthful I swallowed almost stuck in my throat.

"Hello!" I called out, walking over with a smile.

She stood up, clutching the broom to her chest. Her eyes were a pale gray.

"What's your name?" I asked.

Her eyes strayed to the sweets in my hand and then she looked away.

"Do *not* talk to an untouchable!" someone behind me bellowed. "Don't you know it's bad luck for you and for the village? We only speak to give an order. Otherwise, keep your distance and ignore her. It is our way."

6

I whirled round as this ugly word—"untouchable"—bounced in my head. Mr. Venkat stood there, his moustache quivering indignantly. Mom had warned me that the villagers were not only superstitious but also old-fashioned. They still believed in the outdated caste system. Yet, to hear the head of the panchayat speak it so casually and with such conviction made me sick. And furious.

2

This girl was just a kid, like me. The caste system and its horrible labels had been made up by people like Mr. Venkat to make them feel important. In the city, this word and everything it signified had never caught my attention. But here, it was impossible to ignore, loud and shameless—a contagion that touched everything and everyone. I silently thanked Mom for explaining this to me and telling me it was not okay to call anyone by a label or treat them with anything but respect. Besides, who was Mr. Venkat to tell me whom I could talk to, or not?

I wasn't even hungry, and I was gorging myself. She looked like she hadn't eaten a decent meal in days. I held out the sweets to the girl. "Please take this. I'm so full I couldn't eat another bite."

Her smile was sweet and shy. When she looked at Mr. Venkat, her eyes seemed to go black, momentarily. I blinked, and they were a pale gray again. Must have been a trick of the light.

"Get out of here, Lalita," snapped Mr. Venkat. "Come back to clean up when everyone has left."

Before I could say anything, she whirled round and raced off between the tents.

"If you don't know how to uphold tradition, we will teach you, Avi," he said sternly. "When in Tolagunj, you do as *I* say."

I ran after the girl, hoping I'd catch up, but she'd disappeared in the labyrinth of tents and narrow alleys. I shuffled back to the fairgrounds, annoyed with myself, but even more so with Mom. We'd barely arrived, and I'd already been told I would die a horrible death, and whom I should and shouldn't talk to.

Sad.

I walked back to the car. If I could drive, I would have headed to the train station and back home. But arguing with my stubborn mother was useless. Maybe I could work on Dad to take my side.

"What's up, son?" said Dad. He'd been reading the paper, stretched out in the back seat of the car.

"You know what," I said. "I hate it here."

Dad moved over and patted the seat beside him. I climbed in.

"It would make your mother happy if you spent at least a little time with your *nana*. She feels guilty that she did not come back here often enough while your *nani* was alive, and now she wants to remedy it before it's too late. Can't you help her?" Dad was an expert at logical arguments.

"I loved Nani but barely spent any time with her, and now you want me to stay with Nana, whom I know even less," I snapped.

"Then this is the perfect opportunity to get to know him, don't you think?" said Dad. "Plus, it's a good time to catch up on your reading and the story you're working on."

I smiled despite myself. Dad sure knew how to push all the right buttons.

"I would have preferred to stay with Lee," I said. "There's so much more to do in Delhi than here."

"Sometimes we have to do things to make other people happy," said Dad softly. "You'll be on your own for a week and then we'll join you." His brown eyes locked with mine

"Okay," I said with a deep sigh. I couldn't help thinking of the astrologer's dire prediction.

"I noticed a lot of bees and wasps around. Can't be helped since it is summer. But if you use insect repellant and have the EpiPen on you at all times, you'll be fine. You packed the EpiPen, right, Avi?"

"Yes, Dad!" I was about to tell him about the astrologer when Mom hurried up to the car and got in. Dad started the car.

"That Mr. Venkat sure can talk," Mom said when we were on our way.

"He's mean, and he insulted some poor girl, Lalita," I piped in. "He called her an ugly word."

"What do you mean?" asked Mom, turning around to face me in the back seat.

I told her what happened.

Mom grimaced. "Poor Lalita was born into the lowest caste, and no one here will let her forget it."

"If grandfather—Nana—is a powerful man in the village," I said, "why doesn't he educate the people who work his land for him? Surely they would listen to him if he insisted."

Mom sighed. "My father is quite stubborn and set in his ways. It'll take time to change him, if ever."

I liked this less by the minute, but I had no choice. *Serve them both right if I died, and they lost their only child!*

Then I thought of Lee and how he'd think I was being silly. I would have to suck it up and handle seven days on my own. And keep a sharp eye out for wasps.

Mom faced me again. "We had a disagreement, and I stopped talking to both my parents. But after Mother died, I realized time was running—" She stopped and took a shaky breath. "Your nana and nani were very fond of you. I want at least one of them to get to know you better."

"Okay," said Dad. "We're here."

Nana's haveli loomed on the darkening horizon like an ugly toad. A couple of sections of the walls had crumbled away, leaving gaping black holes. Dark green foliage covered the left of the house, as if the haveli were being dragged into the forest but was putting up a good fight.

We zoomed up the driveway and stopped in front of massive wooden doors with a rusting iron ring in the center. The astrologer's prediction pulsed in my head like a red traffic light. The house was far enough from the village that if I screamed for help, no one would come running.

Mom hopped out of the car, climbed the steps, and knocked on the door. I helped Dad get my duffel bag from the trunk. A fist seemed to press down on my chest and I could barely breathe. *Imagination, dude. It's all your imagination.* That is why I was so good at creative writing in class. I would grow up to be a famous writer someday. *If* I survived the next two weeks.

The doors creaked open. Silhouetted in the doorway was a massive person with black eyes and a hooked nose. The tiny mice with icy feet reappeared and raced down my spine as I watched him pluck a wasp off his shirt and crush it with his bare fingers.

3

—————

"Hello, Das," Mom said, smiling at the man. "You haven't changed at all. How have you been?"

"Namaste, Didi, Sahib," Das replied as he brushed bits of wasp from his hand. "Namaste, Avi Baba."

"Hello," I said, eyeing him with disgust and hoping he'd go wash his hands before he touched my bag.

"Das has been with my father since he was a boy," said Mom. "You probably don't remember him, Avi."

"No, I don't," I said. Lucky for me, because he looked like the stuff of nightmares.

We stepped into a gloomy hallway lit by a couple of low-watt bulbs. The smell of wood polish, damp clothes, and sandalwood incense wafted around us. The ceiling disappeared into the darkness above. *One entire week, by myself, in this ancient haveli. Crap.*

I stopped to look at the portrait of Nani hanging in the foyer. She looked kind here, with pale gray eyes and white hair pulled back in a bun. I had a vague recollection of seeing a younger version of that face. Of her singing a tuneless lullaby. I did not know I even remembered her face until now. But I remembered her voice.

The more I stared at the portrait trying to remember Nani, the more it felt as if she were staring at me too. Almost as if she were alive. This wasn't Hogwarts, I reminded myself. I was in an old village in India where people believed in supernatural events and fortune-tellers.

"Please follow me to the kitchen," said Das, lumbering away noisily down the corridor.

I glanced behind me at Nani's portrait. The eyes seemed to have swiveled, following me. I raced back to the picture, but they were staring straight ahead now. *Impossible.*

"Mom, I don't want to stay here," I said as soon as we stepped into the kitchen. "Please."

"Why, Avi Baba?" asked Das. His monobrow wiggled like a furry caterpillar.

I shrugged. "My friends are all back in the city. I'll have nothing to do here." *Nor do I want to die.*

"That is true," said Das. "This is no place for a child."

"Avi has brought books and he can catch up with his nana," said Mom, a slight chill in her voice. "Where is my father?"

"Important work in the village," said Das. "With the panchayat."

Mom looked puzzled. "I met with many people, including Mr. Venkat. I did not see him. Did you see him, Avi?"

I shook my head.

"You have not seen him for ten years," said Das, his voice tinged with reproach. "What's a few more hours? Sit, I will make chai for us all." Lumbering around in the kitchen, Das reminded me of a grizzly bear, though he managed not to knock over and break anything.

"We have a long drive ahead of us," Dad said. "Hold that chai until we are back next week. We'll need it. Come on, Aruna, we better get going."

"Avi, we have to go now," Mom said, looking at me with a worried expression. "We're desperately needed at the hospital in Rajasthan, and I don't have time to make other arrangements."

My friend Lee was an option. One you never considered. I said nothing.

"You have your book, the EpiPen?" Mom continued. "Make sure you have it on you always."

"Aruna, he's twelve, not two," said Dad. "He'll be fine."

Her worried face had me nodding. What else could I do? I would not have a meltdown right now, not with Dad and Das watching. I'd never live it down.

"We'll talk on the phone, every day," Mom said. "The phone line is working, Das?"

"Most of the time, Didi," he said. "Unless we have thunderstorms and heavy rains."

"Avi has his cell phone, Aruna," Dad said. "Come on already."

Mom shook her head. "The cell tower is in the next village and the signal is weak, even in the village. Out here, a cell phone is as good as useless."

I fished out my phone immediately and glanced at it. Not a single bar. I did not like this. *Not at all.* A cell phone without a signal was about as useful as a torn life jacket. I made up my mind to go to the village as often as possible so I could talk to Lee.

"It'll be all right, Avi," she said. "Think of this as an adventure and write about it." She kissed my forehead. "I love you."

"Bye, Mom," I said coldly.

Her mouth drooped. I would not make this easy for her or Dad. They wanted to save lives and be heroes. But what about me? They were abandoning me to strangers!

Dad squeezed my shoulder. "You'll be free of parental supervision for a week. Make the most of it. Go wild."

"Thanks, Dad." I hoped I had the right amount of sarcasm in my voice.

I stood in the doorway as they drove away. The car's lights became red pinpoints in the distance before the darkness swallowed them. Lamp posts beside the gateway spilled watery light on the driveway. The rest of the grounds were in shadowy darkness that rippled outward from the haveli and into the forest.

I felt trapped and more than a little scared.

4

———

"Come," said Das, "I will show you your room. We will have dinner as soon as Sethji gets back."

My room in the attic was shabby, but clean. A musty smell wafted out when Das opened the door, as if no one had used this room in years.

"This was your mother's when she was a child," said Das. "Sethji did not want to change it in case Didi wanted to visit."

No kidding. Pink curtains, pink bedspread, and peeling wallpaper with roses on it. I was probably sleeping on the same mattress she'd used as a kid.

"It's . . . um . . . okay," I said, trying not to grimace.

"Unpack and come to the kitchen," said Das. His footsteps thumped down the stairs and faded away.

I poked my head out the tiny window. Mist swirled around the house, obscuring the lamp posts. I'd never felt so isolated in my life. I checked my phone. Seventy percent battery but no signal. I'd check again when I was in the village. I ranted, silently, for a full minute. At Mom, Dad, Nana, Das, and the universe, as I threw my clothes into a couple of drawers and stacked books beside my bed. The pile looked inviting. So many worlds to dive into so I could forget about this horrible one.

Outside, an owl hooted, making me jump. The noise of the forest grew louder, and I wondered how I would fall asleep without the white noise of traffic. It was so quiet here I could hear my heartbeat. Food smells from the kitchen made my stomach growl in anticipation. The gulab jamuns were a distant memory.

A quick tour of the bathroom revealed modern plumbing. *Yesss!* I washed up and hurried downstairs.

The kitchen slash dining room was the most modern part of the house. Nana probably spent most of his time in here. The walls were a bright red and looked fresh, unlike the rest of the house, which looked faded. A wooden table, polished to a mirror, stood in the center, with uncomfortable-looking wooden chairs all around. A modern cooking range and oven were set against the wall, on which a couple of pots bubbled. I smelled mutton stew and rice. Das puttered around, seasoning the food.

"When do we eat?" I asked. "I'm so hungry."

"As soon as Sethji arrives," said Das. "Neither he nor I like whiners."

Already I didn't like Das. I slid into a chair and fiddled with my cell phone while I waited. Footsteps approached the kitchen, and my heart fluttered. I was seeing my grandfather in person after years. What would he be like?

An old man with thinning silver hair, a kindly wrinkled face, and twinkling eyes entered the room and sat down. "Hello, Avi," he said in a deep but friendly voice.

"Hi, Nana," I said, suddenly shy of this old man who was a complete stranger to me.

"Let me see you properly," he said, gesturing me over.

Nana stared into my face with bright eyes for what seemed like a day. I shuffled my feet. He kissed my forehead gently. His breath smelled of mint toothpaste.

"Welcome to Tolagunj," he said. "It's been far too long. Though I'm not sure now was a good time to come."

"I didn't want to, but Mom insisted," I blurted out.

Nana's eyes bored into my skull, as if trying to root out any lies.

"My Aruna was always headstrong," said Nana with a deep sigh. He slumped a little in his chair. "That's why she left home for a life in the city and never looked back. Is she happy?"

What an odd question to ask me. "Um, yes."

Das finished setting the table. He shifted my placemat next to Nana's, and I slipped into a chair beside him. The ornate wooden spindles dug into my back, but I said nothing.

"Remind me again how long you're staying?" asked Nana, taking a sip of water.

"Two weeks in all. Mom and Dad are helping the relief effort in Rajasthan and they will be back next Sunday. Then we'll all be here for a week."

Nana and Das exchanged a look. What did that mean? Was I welcome or not? *Mom, why did you leave me here?*

"Let's eat," said Nana. "I'm starving, and the stew smells good."

That is one thing we could agree on. "Yes, please."

Das switched on the radio over the mantelpiece. It was the size of an airline carry-on, with a wooden frame and a front of brown cloth with old-fashioned dials. It looked as ancient as Nana, if not more. An announcer was talking about an impending storm before Das switched the station to some dull music. He hurried over to the table and ladled food onto our plates—a mound of fluffy pulao and thick brown mutton stew cascading down its sides. He sprinkled fresh coriander on top with a squeeze of lime juice.

I was about to dig in when someone banged on the door.

"The villagers should know better than to disturb Sethji at dinnertime," said Das, his expression sour. "I'm about to make lassi."

"Shall I get the door?" I asked.

"Thank you, Avi," Nana said. "Tell whoever it is to come back at ten tomorrow morning. That is when I listen to complaints and requests."

I walked through the gloomy corridor lined with portraits. I glanced at Nani but, thankfully, she did not glance back. The musty smell in the corridor lingered. The massive wooden doors were heavy, but I managed to pull one open. Fingers of mist wafted in and curled around the door.

No one was outside. I leaned out and looked to left and right. Zip, zilch, nada. Was this a game of peekaboo? I hoped not. I was starving.

A coppery smell hung in the air. I sniffed hard, trying to figure out where it was coming from. Just then, a flash of lightning tore through the clouds, illuminating something at my feet.

It had a broken neck and was bleeding.

5

I let out a strangled yelp and jumped back. A dead chicken with bloody feathers stared up at me accusingly with a sightless eye.

I slammed the door shut and raced back to the kitchen, heart pounding.

"There's a dead chicken on the doorstep," I yelled. "Is it a death warning?"

"You have a very active imagination, Avi," said Nana. "Why would anyone leave me a dead chicken? Das, please take a look while we finish our dinner."

I'd lost my appetite thinking of the dead chicken oozing blood over the front step. Waiting for Das to come back and confirm what I'd seen, I picked at my food. Classical music blared out from the radio while rain lashed the windowpanes. I tried not to shiver.

Das reappeared after ten minutes. His hair was damp, though his clothes were dry. Had he stepped out to see the chicken, got wet, and changed before he came back to the kitchen? And if he had, why?

"There was nothing on the doorstep, Avi Baba," said Das. "You must be overtired and imagining things."

"No!" I said, looking from him to Nana. "I'll show you the exact spot." I raced to the main door and flung it open with some effort. It was pouring, and the step was wet but devoid of chicken, dead or alive.

Nana peered over my shoulder. Then he guided me back in gently. "This is an ancient village, and sometimes odd and inexplicable things happen here. Don't worry about it too much."

"But . . . but I'm quite certain—"

"Let's go back in and have some tea and dessert," said Nana soothingly.

As we walked back in, I couldn't help recalling the astrologer's warning. And Nani's portrait. Was there something supernatural in this village, or had it been a really long day and my exhaustion was making me imagine things?

"We have a lot to catch up on," said Nana once we sat down again. "Your nani would have been so happy to see you if she were still alive." He stared into the distance.

She'd died last year, and only Mom had attended the funeral. It was exam time and I couldn't miss school. Dad had stayed behind with me.

"I am so sorry," I said, squeezing Nana's hand.

Nana looked at me and smiled sadly. "Thank you, Avi. I miss her every single day. Appreciate your loved ones. You never know when it might be your last day with them."

"Yes, Nana," I said. "Tell me some more about her."

"She was a kind soul and always believed in helping those less fortunate," said Nana. "If she'd had her way, she would have donated all our money to the poor villagers, right, Das?"

Das nodded as he brought masala chai and rice pudding for dessert. I managed a few mouthfuls, unable to get the day's events out of my mind.

"Sometimes I think she wants to talk to me," said Nana suddenly. "I feel like she's trying to reach me."

This was so bizarre I almost choked on my pudding. "How?"

"The dead are resourceful," said Nana. "We only have to provide the means and they will find a way."

I opened my mouth to ask him a question, but an enormous yawn slipped out.

"Better get you to bed," said Nana. "Das, show him to his room, please. I think I'll sit here a while longer and enjoy some music."

"Goodnight," I said, and hurried up the stairs ahead of Das.

Nana was an eccentric old zamindar with terrible taste in music. I understood that he missed Nani, but her wanting to talk to him? That was just silly. And where was that chicken? I could not get that sightless eye out of my mind.

My room was stuffy, so I threw open the window. A cool breeze wafted in. Das pointed to a glass of water sweating by the nightstand. "You have water here already so no need to leave the room," said Das. "Keep the door shut and don't wander around at night. It's not safe, especially since you don't know where everything is. You might fall and hurt yourself."

"Did you really not see the chicken?" I asked Das, hoping he would confess the truth. I knew it hadn't been my imagination.

Das stared at me and shrugged. "Strange things have been known to happen here at the haveli and the village. Don't give it a second thought."

Except that I couldn't not think about it. I looked forward to telling Lee and could almost hear his laughter. Hopefully, tomorrow I'd feel better and forget all about this nonsense.

The bulb was of such low wattage it felt as if I were underwater. Reading in this light would be a strain. I might as well save it until the morning. I undressed, turned off the light, and got into bed. A cool draft blew in from the open window, bringing the scent of wet earth.

The rhythmic tattoo of the rain on the roof lulled me to sleep. I dreamed I was being chased by the astrologer with a chicken's head. A sudden gust of wind blew on his neck, and it snapped and hung at a precarious angle. The girl I'd seen in the market beat him off with a broom, screaming at him to stay away.

I jerked awake and sat up. Someone really was screaming. I threw off the bedcovers and shivered as cool air touched my skin. An orange glow lit up the window, and I hurried toward it, almost tripping over my clothes lying in a heap on the floor. Flames leaped in the distance. Silhouettes carrying buckets of water raced back and forth. Smoke billowed out in thick gray clouds and joined the ones in the sky. The air stank of burning hay and something much worse.

I had to warn Nana and Das in case the fire spread! I raced to the door and tugged it.

It was locked.

Das locked me in? Did Nana ask him to do it, or did Das do this on his own?

I pounded on the door and yelled. No response. What if the haveli caught fire? Would anyone come rescue me? I banged some more and peered through the keyhole. Nothing but blackness beyond.

I hurried back to the window and looked out. The flames seemed to have subsided, and there was more smoke now. I peered down. Vines and creepers covered the wall, but to climb out in darkness would be madness. I'd probably fall and break my leg.

Sleep was out of the question. I stared at my cell phone, willing even a single bar to appear so I could call Mom, Dad, or Lee. Nothing.

I hugged my knees tight and stared at the fire, remembering a painful Diwali when I'd been burned by a firecracker. Alternating between pounding on the door and glancing out the window, I got angrier by the second. I went through every drawer to see if I could find anything to help me escape this room. There was only Nani's picture with Mom. I put that on the nightstand and somehow, inexplicably, I calmed down.

6

A tiny sound outside my door jerked me out of my stupor as I sat by the window. I waited for Das to come in so I could confront him about locking me in, but no one did. After a few minutes, I raced to the door and flung it open. No one was there. If it had been Das, I would certainly have heard him; the man put an elephant to shame when he walked. Who, then? And where had they gone?

As soon as I had freshened up, I marched downstairs and into the kitchen. "Why did Das lock me up in my room last night?" I blurted out. "Also, are you aware there's a fire not too far from here?"

Nana, wearing a fresh white kurta-pajama and an apron with pink elephants, stood by the cooking range, brandishing a spatula. "Fried or scrambled eggs?" he asked. "That's all I can cook. You start the toast."

The sight of Nana in the kitchen offering to cook breakfast was funny, but first things first. "Why was my room locked, Nana? I saw a fire early this morning and wanted to come down to warn you, but I couldn't. I have to call Mom and need to use your phone, please."

Nana studied me, thumping the spatula into the palm of his left hand. "The phone is in my study. You can use it as soon as we finish breakfast. The door to your room gets jammed when it's raining and there's dampness in the air. I'll have Das look at it when he's free. We are aware of the fire—in fact, Das has been helping put it out. He's resting now. Shall we have breakfast?"

I nodded, though I was not buying the stuck-door bit. "How did the fire start? And whose field was it?" I asked.

"Too many questions on an empty stomach are not good for digestion," said Nana. "Let's eat and then we can talk." His tone was cooler, his smile a little strained. I reined in the questions. I still had a week to go and didn't want to annoy him already.

"I'll have scrambled eggs, please." Given my lack of appetite last night, I was ravenous this morning.

Nana cracked eggs into the frying pan. I started making toast. Working side by side, we had an excellent breakfast on the table within fifteen minutes.

"You cook better than Dad," I said, taking a large bite of egg and toast. "This is delicious, thanks!"

"Thank you, Avi." He smiled, his eyes crinkling at the corners. "After my dear Uma—your nani—died, it was just Das and me. On his days off, I had to learn to fend for myself. I miss her."

He sighed so deeply I thought he would cry. But the next minute he was on his feet and reaching for the radio. "How about some music to cheer us up?"

Oh, no, not that ghastly music again.

"Why don't we listen to a different station?" I said, racing to his side. The radio had changed from the one I'd seen yesterday. This one looked modern, with more frequencies.

Just as I reached out, Nana caught my hand in a vise-like grip.

"Please do *not* touch my radio, ever!" he said sternly. "I have set it to the station that Uma listened to, and that must never change. Only Das or I can touch it. Promise that you'll never disobey me, Avi."

Shocked speechless, I didn't reply. Nana snapped his fingers in front of my face. "Pay attention!"

"Yes, okay!" I said, taking a seat again. *Is he all there?*

"Your nani started the radio collection for me," said Nana. "Every year on my birthday, she'd give me one. Some were the latest models, and some were antiques. But no matter which radio, we always listened to this channel. I still do."

"Why?" I asked, not really understanding.

"You never know when Uma will reach out to talk to me, and this is how she will get to me."

"Through the radio?"

"Yes," said Nana.

We ate in silence. I really didn't know what to say to a man who was waiting for his dead wife to talk to him through the radio.

"So, what do you plan to do today?" asked Nana. "Catch up on your reading or sleep? You look tired."

"Explore the village," I said. I desperately needed to talk to Lee and get his take on all these bizarre events.

"I'm sorry, but I can't let you do that," said Nana.

I stared at him. His eyes were kind, but his expression was stern.

"Why not?" I asked.

"Not safe."

"What could happen to me in Tolagunj?"

"You might get run over by a bullock cart. Or a

venomous snake might bite you. The wasps this time of year are vicious," said Nana. "Aruna has told us you're allergic to insect bites."

I stared at him. This was too weird to be a coincidence. The astrologer had told me about wasps. There had been a wasp on Das's kurta and now Nana was also telling me the same thing to keep me inside the house, where I was already feeling claustrophobic.

"I have my EpiPen," I said. "I'll be fine. So, can I go?"

The silence between us stretched. Nana took a sip of tea and hummed along with the music. The repetitive tune had already sawed through my nerves until they were ready to snap.

"Can I at least explore the grounds?" I asked when he still hadn't responded to my question.

He stared at me with concern in his eyes. "Your safety is of utmost importance to me, Avi. Why don't you explore my library? It has an excellent collection of books, many of which were curated by your nani."

If the haveli didn't seem like a prison before, it did now. I made up my mind. No way was I following orders and staying indoors for an entire week. I would explore the grounds at the first opportunity, but I would be careful not to get caught.

As soon as I'd eaten breakfast and helped Nana clear the kitchen, I hurried to his study. It was in an old part of the house and I had to walk through a couple of dimly lit corridors. The floorboards creaked, and the air smelled like damp clothing and stale food. The wallpaper curled away from the walls like potato peels. Something skittered into the darkness as I passed. A cockroach or a mouse. This setting was perfect for a ghost story.

Nana's office door stood ajar. I caught a whiff of sandalwood, which seemed to be his fragrance of choice. I didn't much care about it. There was a massive desk in front of the window, with the chair facing into the room. Beyond the window was a tangle of tall shrubs. The desk was covered with ledgers. The phone sat in one corner, almost drowning in piles of paper.

I picked up the receiver and dialed Mom's number. No response. Dad's cell phone went to voicemail too. They were probably hard at work. Hopefully, they would get my messages and call back. If only I could convince them to come sooner, we could end this boring (and bizarre!) trip and head back to civilization. Not that I believed any of the rubbish Nana or Das spouted. This place was too weird, and I was homesick for normal.

"Did you speak to your mother?" said Nana, walking into the study and settling behind his desk.

"I left a message," I replied.

"I'll try them later too," he said, opening up a thick ledger. "Maybe I'll be able to get through. Now, be a good boy and explore the house. Please do not step outside."

I wandered back through the foyer into the kitchen, thinking about Nana and this haveli. Das still hadn't made an appearance, and the kitchen was empty. I was just about to go find the library when a speck of white outside the pantry caught my eye.

I hurried closer, and my skin crawled. It was a white feather with a bloody tip.

7

I stared at the feather. It belonged to that dead chicken I'd seen last night. I was sure of it. But what was the feather doing here, outside the pantry, and where was the rest of it? Das must have hidden it. Why? Questions swirled in my head like a twig in a whirlpool.

I tugged the pantry door, but it was locked. Why would anyone lock up food? Unless there was more than food inside.

Another mystery to solve in this place. I refused to believe Das or Nana, that strange things happened in this old village. There had to be a more logical explanation, but the chill I felt at seeing the feather was all too real.

I stared at the bright red walls in the kitchen and thought of blood. I had to get out of here and get some fresh air.

I doused myself in insect repellant, patted my pant pocket to make sure the EpiPen was still there, and stepped out of the kitchen door. Fresh air had never smelled so good. A wasp buzzed by my head but did not come too close. I hoped that between the flowers in the garden and the insect spray, I'd be safe.

Just then, I heard Nana talking to someone on the phone. It was so quiet here that voices carried easily. I set out to explore.

I followed a rough path choked with weeds, which ran alongside the haveli. Mosquitoes rose in thick clouds as I walked by. The back of the haveli was shabbier than the front, with exposed bricks and peeling paint. The window in Nana's office, shielded by a row of tall shrubs, was open. I couldn't resist peeking in. Nana must have finished his call and was busy writing in the ledger. He was an odd and fascinating character, and I wanted to know more about him and Das. As I watched, there was a knock on his study door. He looked up. I made sure I was hidden while still being able to peek into the room.

"Come in," Nana called out.

Das, looking tired, entered with a woman following a little distance behind him. She was dark-skinned and wore a shabby white sari. A widow. Her eyes were red and swollen, as if she'd been crying all night.

"Sethji," she sobbed, "I lost everything in the fire! *Everything!* Help me!"

"Shanti, I am so sorry to hear that," said Nana with deep concern in his voice. "Tell me what happened."

I could only see Nana's back, but he sounded genuinely upset with this news.

"I woke up to the sound of breaking glass," the woman said between sobs. "Before I knew what was happening, the flames were all around us. My daughter and I barely escaped with our lives. If only I had listened to that astrologer at the fair . . ." A loud wail and more sobbing drowned her voice.

That astrologer—again! Did he only dole out bad news? Goosebumps freckled my arms as I remembered his prediction for me. I shivered despite the sun scorching my back and glanced around quickly for wasps. There were none in proximity, and I heaved a sigh of relief.

"What did this astrologer say?" asked Nana, leaning forward in his chair.

"He said that if I did not sell you my land and crop immediately, it would be lost. But how could I?" She stopped and wiped the tears streaming from her eyes. "This is *all* I have left to sustain me and my child. Once the land is gone, we'll be on the streets. No one will employ an untouchable to work on a farm."

I felt sorry for her. Some people really had it rough. First she'd lost her husband and now her crops.

"What do you want from Sethji?" Das asked. "Another loan?"

"I need money for food," said the woman, looking from Das to Nana. "Will you still buy my land?"

"The wheat is destroyed," said Das, glaring at her. "If you had accepted Sethji's offer a week ago, we could have come to some decent agreement. You refused. You said you'd sell it over your dead body, and you threw us out of your home. We should do the same to you."

"Shhh, Das," said Nana, standing up and walking around his desk. "One *must* have compassion for the less fortunate. Sister, I will help you and Lalita. That's what I'm here for. We will work something out, and only if you feel you cannot continue working your land, you can come to me and I'll give you a fair price."

My heart swelled with pride. Nana really was a kind and sweet man, despite his oddities. And Das was a villain who needed a serious whack upside his head.

"Go with Das," said Nana. "He will give you food and money to tide you over. Send Lalita to me and I'll give her a job here. At least you will have a steady income."

Shanti fell at his feet. "Thank you for saving me and my family from starvation, Sethji. You are truly a savior."

"He's a fraud but Ma can't see it," said a voice in my ear.

I jumped almost a foot in the air and turned to find a girl crouching beside me.

8

I'd been so intent on eavesdropping that I hadn't heard her creep up. She wore a patched kurta-pajama and a white dupatta. Where had I seen her before? *Where?* Then I remembered—her name was Lalita, and I'd offered her sweets at the market, but she'd run off when Mr. Venkat arrived. What was she doing *here*?

"Who are you talking about?" I asked.

"Sethji," she said, massaging her temples, eyes downcast.

"Why?" I said. "My grandfather is helping by offering food and money."

"We don't need his help," she said. Her pale gray eyes seemed to look through me.

"You're that woman's daughter!" I said as I made the connection.

She nodded. "If Ma accepts his help, we'll be trapped. I have to stop her."

"Wait!" I said, grabbing her shoulder. "Let's figure this out before you barge in." I didn't know why, but I was sorry for Lalita and wanted to help her. Das was sure to belittle her and throw her out.

"You're breaking the rules by touching me," she said, moving away.

"Sorry," I said, blushing. "I didn't want you to run away like last time. You're Lalita, aren't you? I'm Avi."

"Please don't touch me again. If anyone sees us, you'll only get a scolding. Ma and I will be severely punished."

Mr. Venkat's words came back to me. All the other pieces were coming together as well. "So, the field that burned down was yours and everyone treats you badly because you were born in a . . . lower caste." Saying this out loud made me cringe.

"They try," said Lalita with a defiant look. "I've learned to ignore them. When they don't get a reaction, they move on. But Ma still gets upset, wishing she could give me a better future."

Das must have heard us talking because he looked at the window. I grabbed Lalita's hand, and we slipped away to the sheltered gazebo I'd passed along the way. The shrubs and weeds around it were so overgrown they formed a natural wall on three sides. Lalita collapsed on a bench, holding her head in her hands. She looked tired and hungry.

"Wait here," I said. "I'll be right back."

I hurried into the kitchen and grabbed some food: a couple of apples, a leftover paratha, and a bottle of water. I raced back and handed the food to Lalita.

She devoured it, almost choking. Watching her, I realized how lucky I was—I'd never been this hungry, *ever*, in my life.

"Thank you," she said when she'd finished.

"What now?" I asked.

"We may have to leave the village," she said, pacing in the tiny space. "I wish Sethaniji were still alive. I loved her."

"You mean Nani?"

Lalita nodded, her eyes moist. "Her heart was full of love. She never made me feel small and always had a kind word for me. I felt a special connection to her."

I couldn't help but think of Nani's portrait in the haveli and how her eyes had seemed to follow me. "What do you mean?" I asked.

Lalita shrugged. "It's hard to explain." The sun caught her eyes then, and they reminded me of Nani's. They were a similar shade of gray.

"You have been very kind to me too," said Lalita. "So, a word of advice: be careful. This place is not safe for you. You should leave as soon as you can."

This was bizarre. First the astrologer had warned me, and now Lalita. Was this some elaborate prank, or was I really in danger? I touched my EpiPen again, just in case. It was still there in my pocket. "What?" I choked out. "Why?"

A twig snapped close by.

"Who's there?" I called out, my pulse racing.

I peered out of the gazebo, Lalita at my shoulder. The bushes, a short distance away, sprang into place, as if someone had just passed by. There was a faint buzzing in the distance.

"Did you see who that was?" I whispered to Lalita.

She looked worried as she shook her head. "I could get into trouble just for talking to you. You better go before we're seen together."

"Lalita!" a woman called out just then. "Come, child, let's go."

"That's Ma," said Lalita. "You go on ahead, and I'll follow."

We skirted a pond beside the gazebo that I hadn't noticed before. It was choked with weeds and would have been impossible to spot from a distance. The center was murky. I'd never liked swimming in a body of water where I couldn't see the bottom. I'd made the mistake of watching the movie *Jaws*. Twice.

The buzzing grew louder and suddenly a black cloud swarmed around the side of the haveli and whooshed toward us.

"Oh, no!" I yelled. "I'm allergic." I scrabbled for my EpiPen in my pocket and finally took it out. My heart almost burst out of my chest in shock. It was a pen all right—a regular ballpoint pen. Someone had switched it.

I was going to die!

9

Lalita shoved me into the pond and dived in, pulling me under. I would have yelled, but my nose was full of cold, stinking mud and rotten leaves.

Mud oozed into my mouth as I gasped for breath. Choking, spluttering, I tried to get to the surface. I almost made it when Lalita dragged me down again.

My lungs were bursting, but I had two options: drown or get bitten to death.

I decided to go with bitten; at least I'd be able to get in one last lungful of air. I shook off Lalita's grasp and shot to the surface. The moment I broke through the water, a loud buzzing filled my ears. Wasps circled overhead, the air thick with their yellow-black bodies. A couple of them stung my face and neck. It felt like someone had stabbed me. I waved my hands in the air, swatting them away.

"Deep breath, Avi," said Lalita, and pulled me down again.

I sank below the surface, the cool mud taking the edge off the stings. The pond was shallow, and I could kneel on the bottom. Slimy plants coiled around my arms and legs.

Mud oozed into my ears, eyes, mouth. My heartbeat was loud in my ears.

Where had all those wasps come from? I'd only seen a few in the garden. This looked like someone had disturbed a whole nest.

I was blacking out, but I stayed under, counting back from a hundred. After what seemed like a million years, but must have been a minute at the most, Lalita raised her head above the surface.

She dragged me up a second later. "They're gone. You're safe."

I finally gulped in air, shaking all over.

By the time we pulled ourselves out of the pond, Das, Nana, and Shanti had arrived.

"What happened?" asked Nana, looking white. "I thought I told you to stay indoors. What are you doing in this filthy pond with—"

He did not finish the sentence, but I knew what he meant.

"Wasps!" I said, touching my fingertips to the stings on my face and neck. "They came out of nowhere. If Lalita hadn't been there, they would have stung me to—" I stopped. *Death*.

"No one dies of a wasp sting," said Das with a sneer. "Stop being melodramatic."

"You do if you're allergic and someone has switched your EpiPen with a ballpoint pen!" I glared at Das, but he said nothing.

Nana hugged me close, despite my filthy, sodden clothes. "I'm sorry you had such a scare, Avi. Do you want to call Aruna? I will understand if you don't want to stay here. This is no place for a child, especially one with severe allergies."

I wanted to leave, badly. But now I had to prove that

39

superstitions and supernatural things just did not exist. There had to be another explanation for all these weird incidents. If I left, I'd never know. I wanted to sort this out. I *had* to.

"I'm all right," I said. "It's only a matter of a few days, and Mom and Dad will be here on Sunday."

"I want you to be safe," said Nana. "Aruna would never forgive me if something happened to you. It's a good thing you jumped into the water. Mud will help reduce the pain and swelling. You should also take a dose of your medicine. Do you have another EpiPen?"

"I'm okay," I said. And I was. Luckily, I must have got only two bites and no severe allergic reaction had set in. I wasn't in anaphylactic shock. "You can thank Lalita for that. It was her quick thinking that saved us."

No one said a word for an entire minute. Lalita and her mother shifted uneasily, edging away from us.

I noticed Das's expression. He looked angry and sly at the same time as he scratched his arms, trying not to draw attention to them. "You should listen to Sethji," he said. "Maybe it's best if you go home."

"Let's all go in," said Nana. "I'm sure Avi needs to change into something warm and dry."

Lalita and her mother turned to go.

"Wait!" I stuck out my hand toward Lalita. "Thank you for saving my life!"

Mother and daughter both turned white. Their gaze went to Das and Nana as they backed away. "It was my duty," said Lalita in a low voice. "No need for thanks."

"Please go now," said Nana. "I will visit you tomorrow and we can finish our discussion."

I was white-hot on the inside. Lalita had saved my life, but she could not accept thanks because of old customs and traditions still in practice in Tolagunj. Neither Nana nor Das had thanked her either.

"Yes, there is a need, Lalita," I said. "Thank you for saving my life."

Back inside, Nana went to his office, and I headed upstairs to bathe and change. I couldn't resist a peek over the banister at Das, who was still in the foyer. He'd pulled up the sleeve of his kurta and was furiously scratching three large welts on his arm.

They looked like wasp bites, just like mine.

10

A second EpiPen was in my duffel bag and I took a dose just to be on the safe side. The mud bath had acted as a natural suppressant, but I didn't want to take any chances. I had been incredibly lucky to have the quick-thinking Lalita with me.

After a bath, I tried to read but when I'd gone through the same paragraph three times and still didn't have a clue what it said, I tossed the book aside. Something was wrong with Das, and Nana did not have a clue. I was desperate to talk to Lalita and ask her more about this village astrologer. His prediction about Lalita's field had come true. The prediction that I would die a horrible death by wasps had *almost* come true. Who would be the next to die? More importantly: what could I do about it?

I tried to call Mom and Dad again. They didn't pick up their phones. Did they not care about me at all? Even though I knew they were busy helping the sick, I was mad at them for leaving me here. I was tempted to call Lee and ask him to come over with his mom and pick me up. Nana would probably let me go, but Mom would be angry. She'd probably ground me for the rest of my life.

I had to stay and get to the bottom of all this. Running away was not the solution. There had to be a more rational explanation to all this. The bites on Das's arm were a good start. Somehow, he was involved in the wasp attack, of that I was sure.

Back in my room, I stood by the window. Thick creepers covered the entire front of the house, almost up to the roof. A few tendrils of green hung down past the window frame. I could climb down if there was an emergency. That thought gave me little comfort. Even if I got to the ground, it was still a long way to Delhi.

A MOVEMENT CAUGHT MY EYE. Lalita was sweeping through the courtyard. She must have changed and come back to work. At least Nana had kept his word about giving Lalita a job. I admired him for that.

This was my chance to talk to her. Trembling, I flung a leg over the sill. The vines looked strong, and I hoped there was nothing dangerous lurking in the foliage. Like a king cobra. Or a venomous spider. Or even more wasps. The spots where the wasps had got me were still tender.

I waved to Lalita, gesturing that I was coming down. She shook her head, but I ignored her.

Slowly, carefully, I inched down the vines. Twice, a thick strand broke under my weight. I slid down a few inches, my stomach jumping into my throat each time. I forced myself to hang on and breathe.

It felt like hours before I stepped onto solid ground.

"You're careless," whispered Lalita. "You could have broken your neck."

"I have to talk to you," I said, leading the way to the cowshed beside the haveli. Two plump cows munched on hay and ignored us.

"I need your help," I blurted out as soon as we were inside. "The astrologer at the fair predicted I would die of wasp bites if I stayed here. You warned me to be careful too. I don't believe in all this stuff. Either it's a lucky guess or a coincidence."

"I believe in all this 'stuff', as you call it," said Lalita in a distant voice. "So did Sethaniji."

I shrugged, not wanting to get into an argument with her. "But my nani is not here, and the astrologer is. I really need to see him again and ask him some more questions."

A cow mooed softly and ambled toward the water trough. It was such a normal setting: a rural village, cows, a crumbling haveli. Yet something sinister lurked just below the surface. I was determined to find out what that was.

"If the astrologer can predict bad things, why not good ones?" I asked. "Better yet, why not predict ways to avoid the terrible events?"

"If I knew, I would not have lost my crop, would I?" said Lalita, her eyes darting to the entrance. No doubt she was nervous about Das.

"I'm sorry, Lalita. You've been through a lot and I'm being selfish. Please help me find this astrologer."

"He's usually at the Sunday market," said Lalita. "You'll have to wait till then."

"Do you have any idea how the fire in your field started?" I could not get that blazing field, the acrid smell, and the black smoke out of my mind. I'd spent last night locked in my room, scared to death. "I'm going to solve the mystery of the fire, the wasps, and especially the astrologer. Will you help me?"

She gazed at me, terrified but also surprised. "Me, help you? You must know by now that everyone in the village hates us. No one will even *look* at me, let alone talk to me."

"That's perfect," I said. "You can sneak around and observe people, and no one will notice you. Unfortunately, I can't even leave the house, let alone go to the village. You do not know how lucky you are."

Lalita's eyes were like pebbles. "You think I'm *lucky* to be an untouchable?" Her lips were peeled back in a snarl. Her eyes bulged and her fists were clenched, as if she was about to throw a punch at me. I took a step back. I'd never seen her this angry. It hit me then—I'd said something incredibly thoughtless.

"I'm so sorry, Lalita. That was the silliest thing I've ever said. Please let me explain?"

She shoved me hard. "Get out of my way," she snapped.

"Please, at least tell me why you're so angry," I said. "I know it's a bad thing to be an untouchable—"

She whirled around and brought her face close to mine. Tears filled her eyes. "Do you have any idea what it is like to be ignored, hated, yelled at, and taunted every waking moment of your life? To have people think you are so unclean that they have to purify the place with prayers after you have walked by?"

I stared at her, shocked. I did not know it was this bad. She continued, as if a dam had burst inside her.

"Do you know what real hunger is?" she said, her eyes blazing. "Hunger so bad that even spoiled food tastes amazing? No, Avi. *You do not.* Being who I am is not 'lucky'. It's a curse I was born with and will have to live with the rest of my life."

"Do you have friends whom you can turn to for help?"

"There used to be two other families like ours in the

village. We'd look after each other when times got tough. They moved away last year to the city, and now it's just Ma and I."

I couldn't imagine how hard it must be to have everyone hate you, treat you like garbage just because of the label given to you at birth. "How do you handle all this without exploding?"

"Ma and I keep our heads down and get through day by day. As soon as we have enough money, I'm going to the city too and I'm taking Ma with me."

Words failed me. I hadn't realized how bad things were for people like Lalita and her mother.

"I'm so sorry," I said, feeling like crying. "Can you please forgive me, Lalita?"

Lalita swiped at the tears on her cheeks. She went up to a cow that had stopped eating and was watching us with soft brown eyes. She stroked its nose, and it nuzzled close.

"You know why I love animals more than people?" she whispered.

I stood beside her. "No, why?"

"They don't judge you based on who you are or where you were born."

"I would never do that, Lalita! I can't change your life, but if we solve the mysteries you can get paid for what you lost. Nana knows you saved my life. I'll even tell Mr. Venkat when I see him. Maybe people will stop mistreating you after that."

Lalita was silent for a while. I stayed quiet too, her words churning in my head. What an insensitive fool I'd been.

"Okay, I'll help," said Lalita. "What do you want me to do?"

"Find out where the astrologer lives or does business for the rest of the week. If we can, somehow, see him, we can get answers faster. Even if we can observe him, we can plan on how to expose him."

She nodded.

"I have a bad feeling about Das," I continued. "I think he's taking Nana for granted and may end up robbing or harming him. Nana is old and not as strong as he used to be."

Lalita looked troubled. I got the feeling she wanted to say something but was holding back. She looked at me, finally, her eyes apprehensive. "Sometimes, the truth only creates more problems. Can you really handle the truth?"

I met her gaze. "Yes."

11

A slimy piece of seaweed wrapped itself around my mouth. I couldn't talk or breathe. I thrashed wildly, trying to escape.

"Shhh," said a soft voice. "It's me, Lalita."

Moonlight poured into my room from the open window. Lalita crouched beside my bed, her hand on my mouth. I'd been having a nightmare, and she'd woken me at the right time.

"I have news," she whispered. "Hurry and get dressed. I'll meet you outside." She climbed out the window and a faint rustling marked her progress to the ground.

I climbed down and was standing beside her in under a minute. Not bad for a city person, if I thought so myself.

"What's going on?" I asked.

"We're going to Venkat's place," said Lalita.

"The head of the panchayat, Venkat?" I asked.

"Yes," said Lalita. "I was sweeping in the market square when I heard Venkat talking to the village grocer. The astrologer had predicted that he should buy a spare cow in case something happened to the one he had. The astrologer said it did not have long to live and, with harvest season around the corner, he should have a spare. Venkat complained that cows cost too much, and the astrologer had suggested a loan. From your grandfather."

"Okay," I said. "What's the plan when we get there?"

"We snoop around," said Lalita, "and we also keep an eye on the cow. Odd things have happened in Tolagunj, and this time we might witness it."

"Please, Lalita, not you too." All this talk of the supernatural was getting to me. There was no such thing and no matter who said it or how many times, I refused to believe in it.

Her eyes seemed to glow silver in the light from the lamps. I blinked, and they looked normal again. Must have been the trick of the light. No way was Lalita glowing from the inside.

"We're wasting time," she said. "Let's go."

The night was chilly, and a full moon slipped through the clouds. I stuck close to Lalita, who was sure-footed and silent. I sounded like a rhino in comparison. A cool wind set the leaves trembling and sighing. An owl hooted. Another answered. The sound of crickets stopped, started again. The smell of earth and rotting leaves wafted up to us as we took a shortcut through the forest to the village.

"When did you overhear this conversation?"

"This morning," said Lalita, picking up the pace.

This astrologer made the worst predictions ever—all doom and gloom. How great would it be if he predicted someone was coming into money or was going to have a baby? But no, I had not heard a single positive thing since I'd arrived at the village. I did not know how, but it was time to find this guy and stop him, or make the predictions more positive.

We passed through the village, which looked like a ghost

town this late at night. The smells of food lingered in the cool air, mixed with the smoke from wood fires and kerosene lanterns. Shadows lurked in the alleyways and my heart leaped in my throat each time until I realized it was only the village strays.

"How much farther?" I said, rubbing my cold arms.

"Venkat has the largest house in Tolagunj, but it's a little farther away from the rest of the houses to give him privacy," said Lalita.

As we crept up to Venkat's house, we slowed down, looking for signs of anyone who might be awake. No one stirred, and the house was dark. The air stank of fresh dung. We peeked over the low wall of an enclosure where a white cow was tethered. She munched on grass, the bell around her neck tinkling softly as she moved.

"All clear," said Lalita.

As we stepped over the wall, the cow came over and nudged me with a wet nose. It was gross and sweet at the same time. I stroked her forehead, the skin rough under my fingertips.

"That's a good place to hide," I said, pointing to a spot under a tree with deep shadows, a short distance away from the enclosure.

We crept to the base of the tree and huddled between its twisted roots. An hour passed, then two. The night chill deepened, and I shivered involuntarily. The fragrance of a sweet flower tickled my nose.

"What is that?" I said, sniffing hard.

"Jasmine," said Lalita. "Don't talk. Someone else could also be hiding, watching *us*."

She was smart, cool, and brave. How could anyone not see that? "Okay," I whispered.

We sat close, arms touching. Her clothes were threadbare, but she seemed not to feel or mind the cold. I wished something would happen *soon*. Then I could go back to my warm bed. I stopped and berated myself silently. *How can I think of myself when an innocent animal is in danger? When Lalita lost her crop and is facing starvation?* I was being selfish. I gritted my teeth and hunkered down.

Another half hour crawled by. My teeth were chattering. Lalita was shifting and rubbing her arms too. A snake tongue of lightning licked the sky. A thunderclap followed. *Great!* Rain was just what we needed to cheer us up. The cow mooed. I needed to pee, but this would be TMI as far as telling Lalita.

"We should go—" I started to say.

"Someone's coming," Lalita whispered, cutting me off.

A figure crept up to the water trough. A blanket covered the face, and it was hard to see the person's face. My heart galloped as if I'd run a marathon. I clutched Lalita's hand as we watched, barely breathing.

The figure seemed too large to be a woman, so, most likely, it was a man. He reached into the folds of his loose trousers. Paper rustled. He poured the contents into the trough, dunked his hand in and sloshed the water around.

"STOP!" I said, jumping to my feet involuntarily.

The man startled and raced off, blanket flapping in the breeze. I sprinted after him, Lalita right behind me. He was quick and sure-footed. I tripped over a tin bucket, which crashed against the shed, shattering the silence. *Crap!*

Someone called out from within the house. "Who's there? You're trespassing!"

"Are you all right?" asked Lalita, helping me to my feet.

My shin throbbed, but I nodded. "I'm fine. Did you see where he went?"

"No, but now you've woken Venkat up," she said, looking terrified. "He will not be happy seeing us—*me*—here."

The villagers' unkindness terrified her more than anything. "I'm sorry for being so clumsy," I said. "I should have been more careful. Listen, you run and hide. I'll tell Venkat I was here all alone. I'm good at making up stories."

"Too late," she said.

Venkat stumbled toward us, lantern in hand and rubbing sleep from his eyes. He spat on the ground when he saw Lalita and kept his distance. His eyes widened when he saw me. "You're the zamindar's grandson. Why are you sneaking around my property like a thief?"

"I can explain—"

"What are *you* doing here, you filthy untouchable?" he snapped, cutting me off. "How dare you come this close to my house?"

Lalita hung her head, wringing her hands, as if she knew she was in deep trouble. I glared at him. The anger bubbling up inside me at Venkat's rudeness took the edge off the chill.

"We came to *protect* your animal!" I said. "You should thank us instead of yelling at us."

He stepped closer and yawned. A foul odor wafted from his mouth. "Explain!"

"We heard the astrologer suggested you buy another cow," I said, taking a step back. "That this one might not survive. We came to see if we could stop it."

"That's none of your business, or Lalita's," he snapped. "I'm perfectly capable of looking after my property. If my wife sees you, she'll insist on a costly purification ceremony of not only the house but the entire grounds. More expenses that I cannot afford."

Steam was probably shooting out of my ears. Lalita, on

the other hand, remained calm despite being insulted to her face. She must have had years of practice.

"We saw someone mix something in the water," Lalita said, pointing to the trough. "Empty it before any of the livestock drink it."

Venkat snorted. "Rubbish. This is a good excuse to trespass. Maybe steal something to sell in the next village?" He eyed Lalita. "I know your field burned down."

"I am poor, but I'm *not* a thief!" she said, her voice quivering.

My hands clenched into fists. I wanted to punch Venkat on the nose. Or dunk his head in the trough. "She's telling the truth," I said. "Do you want your cow to die?"

"You really came to watch over the cow, not steal something?"

"Yes," I said, giving him a stink eye.

He believed *me* instead of Lalita. She truly was invisible. If I'd had the bad luck to be born in Tolagunj to a lower caste family, this could have been my fate. This had to stop, and Nana was the key.

Venkat shuffled to the trough, holding the lantern high. He sniffed the water, hesitating. I understood his reluctance to throw the water away. Water was precious, and we were asking him to waste at least ten liters based on "someone put something into it". I could see that he sort of believed me. As far as Lalita's warning went, he'd given it as much importance as a pile of dung.

The cow ambled toward the trough. Lalita jumped into action, grabbing the rope around the cow's neck. "Water!" she yelled out.

I knew exactly what she meant and overturned the trough. *Let them scream at me instead of her.*

"Hai, Ram!" gasped Venkat, thumping his forehead. "This better not be a joke or your grandfather will pay for it."

I was getting tired of his suspicious nature even though we'd just saved his cow. I was sure that whatever the intruder had mixed into the water, it wasn't vitamins. "Fine. Talk to him tomorrow."

We turned to go, but Venkat barked out an order. "Before you go, Lalita, wash the trough and refill it from the well."

"Why me?" she asked, her eyes flashing. For the first time tonight, I saw she was livid. Her voice shook. "Avi was the one who emptied it."

"Because I *told* you to do it," Venkat said. "The only reason you're still allowed to live in the village is because you obey orders. Are you refusing to do as I say?"

Wow! "How dare you—" I said.

"It's fine," said Lalita, cutting me off. "I wasn't expecting anything but this from him."

This was so unfair that my gut burned with the words I was dying to spit into Venkat's face. I insisted on helping, even though Venkat and Lalita both protested. As we worked, side by side, I wished I could make the villagers change their opinions about Lalita. She was smart, helpful, and kind.

Even more burning than that was the desire to find the astrologer and put a stop to his predictions. I would not rest, or leave, till I discovered the truth.

12

The next morning, raised voices wafted up from the kitchen. It sounded like Venkat. I dressed hurriedly and raced downstairs, still fuming over his treatment of Lalita. *We should have let his cow die.* But I knew I couldn't have done that, no matter how cranky its owner.

Venkat sat at the table, a cup of tea before him, looking very upset.

"Good morning, Avi," Nana said. "You know Venkat, our head of panchayat."

"Morning, Nana, and yes, I know him."

Venkat poured some tea in a saucer and took a big slurp, his eyes not leaving my face. "No-good rascals, both your grandson and that untouchable."

"Now, now, Venkat," said Nana sternly. "This is my family you're insulting, in my house. You will stop immediately."

"My cow is dead because of them," Venkat spat out. "She was a family member, and these two killed her!" He thumped the table with his fist, making the cups rattle.

I wanted to barf even though I'd not eaten anything

since last night. *Dead? But we'd saved her, and spent another hour refilling the water trough.*

Nana shook his head sorrowfully. "I am sorry to hear that, Venkat. Cows are our mothers." He folded his hands, closed his eyes, and said a brief prayer.

"How are you going to punish this boy?" said Venkat. "That girl too."

I ignored him and addressed Nana. "We were only trying to help. We saw a man tip something into the trough, so we emptied the water. Venkat made us fill it before he threw us out. I don't know what happened after that. You *have* to believe me."

"Why were you at Venkat's house at all?" Nana asked me. His quiet voice scared me even more than if he'd yelled at me. "Did I not tell you not to leave the house, especially after the incident with the wasps? I am very disappointed in you, Avi."

I shoved my trembling hands into my pocket. I wished Mom and Dad were here. I had to face an angry headman, and Nana, who was still a stranger, with no one to back me up. Neither believed I was telling the truth. Then I thought of Lalita, who always put on a brave face no matter how unfair the situation. It gave me strength to speak up.

"The astrologer at the fair has been making terrible predictions and most of them have come true," I said. "He'd predicted I would die because of wasp bites. Luckily, I didn't. I am determined to find out if these are coincidences or if there is something that I'm missing."

I was watching Das. His eyes slid away from me, and he looked shifty. Nana spoke to me. "Avi, you come from the city, so this may be hard to believe, but there are many unexplainable occurrences in Tolagunj. It's an ancient village and these things happen in a place with a lot of history.

Only a few wise ones, like the astrologer, can see the future. The villagers respect him and his predictions. You should too."

"Has he made any predictions for you?" I asked Nana. "Have you met him? In fact, summon him here so that we can question him together."

Nana smiled. "Wise men cannot be summoned at whim. And no, I have not yet had my fortune told. Maybe I will next time."

None of this talk seemed to surprise Das. He knew something, of that I was sure.

"I need more livestock to plough the fields," said Venkat. "But I'm short of funds right now. Maybe another small loan?" He looked at Nana. "I will repay it all with interest when I have a good crop."

"Of course, Venkat," said Nana. "How could I refuse a loan to the head of the panchayat? But your existing debt is quite substantial. I will need some collateral. It's a mere formality but, alas, I have to keep my books balanced."

"Of course," said Venkat. "Anything you say. We both know you will never collect."

Nana was too kind for his own good, and even Venkat was taking advantage of him. I wished I could have a private chat with Nana to clear all the questions and also warn him about Das.

"What about his punishment?" said Venkat, glaring at me.

I had hoped he might have forgotten, but I wasn't that lucky.

"He can clean out the cowshed," said Nana. "Das, get him started after breakfast."

Nana strode away with Venkat trailing behind him like an obedient dog. As soon as they were out of sight, Das gripped my arm and shoved me into a chair. I hit my elbow on the armrest and pain shot up my arm. Arrogance had replaced his simpering demeanor.

I watched him make breakfast, trying to recall the stranger I had seen last night. The longer I looked, the more it bothered me. I kept trying to push the thought away, but there it was, front and center. Das was the key to this mystery, and I was going to solve it. I wished Lee were with me. His ideas were genius. But instead of Lee, I had Lalita, and we had to figure this out on our own.

I drummed my fingers on the table while Das cooked. My gaze wandered to the radio. With a tiny jolt I realized, once again, it was a new one. Thankfully, it was off. I could do without the screeching of instruments while my brain went into hyperdrive trying to put together the pieces of the puzzle.

Das left while I was still eating. As soon as his footsteps died away, I raced outside and tiptoed to Nana's office, using the path behind the house, keeping a wary eye out for wasps. The shutters were drawn. Nana and Das were talking too softly for me to hear anything. Venkat seemed to have left.

I hurried back to the kitchen. This was my chance to find out more about the dead chicken. I tiptoed to the pantry and tugged. To my delight, it was unlocked. I pulled the door open and peered inside. Answers, at last! The shelves were lined with tins of flour, lentils, biscuits, and assorted pickles. The smell of masalas was overpowered by the heady scent of ripening Alphonso mangoes in straw-filled baskets on the floor.

Nothing seemed out of place. I was about to leave when a sliver of light at the far end caught my eye. I hurried toward it.

A locked door. I jiggled it, but it didn't budge. I got down on all fours and peered at the gap under the door. Stone steps leading down. To where? And why was the entrance to it hidden inside the pantry? I realized there was so much more to the haveli than met the eye.

"What are you doing, Avi?" a voice thundered.

I jumped to my feet, knocking a jar of pickled chillies off the shelf. It shattered, and shards of glass flew everywhere. The smell of vinegar filled the small space, making my eyes water.

Das filled the doorway, glaring at me. "Now look what you've done!" he said in a low, menacing voice. "That was my last jar from two summers ago. Poking your nose where you shouldn't."

My heart quivered. "It was an accident," I said as I hurried to the door and tried to slip past him, back into the kitchen. "What if it had fallen on my foot? I could have been badly hurt."

"I asked you a question," he said, clamping his meaty hand around my wrist. His fingertips dug into my flesh and the pain took my breath away. Das was *really* scaring me now.

"*What* are you doing in here?" His black eyes looked murderous.

My brains scurried for an answer. "I was hungry and wanted a mango."

"The mangoes are by the door; you were way inside, there," said Das. "Plus, you just ate breakfast. You're lying."

Sharp cookie.

"I saw a chicken feather outside the pantry the other day," I said, deciding that bravado and the truth might work better. "You said there was nothing on the doorstep when you went to check but I think *you're* lying."

Das chuckled. "Really?" he said, towering over me. "If you don't stop poking your nose where it doesn't belong, you'll end up like that chicken. The astrologer's prediction might come true, with a little help from me."

It felt as if someone had reached inside my chest with icy hands and squeezed my heart. Das had just threatened me. This man was dangerous and mad. The pantry stank of vinegar, sweat, and stale BO.

I took a shaky breath but held my ground. "There's a door leading down to the cellar. What's behind it?"

"Extra food and the bodies of my victims." Das took a step closer, grasped my shoulders, and squeezed. "Want to see?"

I let out an involuntary gasp. "Let go! You're hurting me."

"What are you both doing in there?" said Nana from the kitchen.

"I was letting Avi Baba choose a mango to have after lunch," said Das, his voice oily again. "Isn't that right?"

"Good, good," said Nana absently. "Come with me, Das. I have some work for you. Avi, you will clean the cowshed as punishment for disobeying me. Then go up to your room and stay there. Under no circumstances are you to leave the grounds to go anywhere. Are we clear on that?"

I nodded and Nana walked away, the sound of his footsteps on the tiled floor receding.

"Be careful, Avi," said Das. "There are many ways to die. If I were you, I'd call your parents and leave as soon as possible."

I shot past Das, and this time he made no move to stop me. I wondered if he had been the intruder at Venkat's. The more I thought about it, the more it made sense. If I wasn't careful, he'd murder Nana and me both while we slept.

There had been many cases in Delhi where people, especially elders, were betrayed by those closest to them.

The kitchen was gloomy. Lightning whipped the thunderclouds waddling across the sky. The wind howled through the trees.

I had to be smarter than this hulk and find a way to keep us both safe until Mom and Dad returned. How would I do that when Das always hung around us like a bad smell?

13

After I'd finished cleaning the cowshed, which was gross, I hurried through the pouring rain and back up to my room. I slammed the door when I got in and tried to lock it. To my shock, the bolt had disappeared. I stared at the strip of dark wood where it should have been. Had it been there when I'd arrived? I couldn't remember. I'd not needed to lock the door before, but now it was a matter of life and death. The one on the outside—a simple slide bolt—was still there.

So, Das could lock me in, but I could not lock him out.

My head pounded with questions as I paced the room. What if Das came in the middle of the night and murdered me? Why had he been at Venkat's place? Was he in cahoots with the astrologer and was Nana the next target?

I had to talk to Nana ASAP and tell him that Das was dangerous. Plus, I needed proof that Das was connected with the astrologer or that he had evil intentions. Without proof, no one would believe that Das was up to no good while pretending to be a loyal servant. The only way was to keep a close eye on Das and record him in action. I'd have to make sure the phone was charged at all times.

I wandered over to the window. The rain had stopped momentarily, but black clouds filled the horizon and tendrils of lightning trailed between them like the tentacles of a giant octopus. A figure, holding a tattered umbrella, hurried into the cowshed I had just mucked out. Lalita. I had to talk to her.

I made sure the coast was clear and raced down. She was in a corner of the shed, mixing straw into the dung and making dung cakes for the fire. It was a disgusting job, and it made sense that Das would pass it on to someone else.

"Are you okay?" I asked.

Lalita startled but settled down when she realized it was only me. "Please go away and don't talk to me. You'll get me into trouble and I can't afford that right now."

"I came to apologize. Nana punished me too, if you must know."

Lalita said nothing as she slapped the dung patties onto the wall. They stuck there and would stay there till they dried. The smell was awful, but I did not mind. At least I had someone to talk to.

"I think something weird is going on," I said. "I need your advice."

Lalita looked up and opened her mouth to say something, but no words came out. Someone blocked the weak daylight coming in, and even before I turned around, I knew who it was.

"You're done here," said Das. "Leave now and don't come back."

"Please!" begged Lalita. "I need this job, or my mother and I will starve."

Watching Das bully my friend made me want to punch him.

"Not my problem," said Das. "Go to the city like your

63

friends did. Less garbage in Tolagunj, and you'll find more work there."

"How can you be so cruel?" I said, stepping between him and Lalita. "Do you get pleasure in bullying kids?"

Das pushed me aside and dragged Lalita out of the shed and into the courtyard. Her lip quivered and her eyes filled with tears.

I felt like crying too.

Thunder crashed overhead. A terrible storm was almost upon us, and Lalita would have to walk home through the fields, where she might get hit by lightning. My stomach clenched at the thought. I would have invited her up to my room to wait out the storm, but it would be impossible with Das barring the way.

"Go!" said Das.

"Stop it!" I yelled.

The front door opened, and Nana stood inside. "Das, what is all this ruckus? Why is Avi yelling? Can't I get any peace around here?"

"He fired me, Sethji," said Lalita, racing over to him and touching his feet. "I've done nothing wrong. I need this job. Please let me keep working, or my mother and I will starve."

Nana took a step back. I cringed. He was kinder than Das, but he still believed in the caste system and kept his distance from Lalita. How could one human treat another so badly?

"Please don't fire her," I said. "She's smart and kind and she saved my life."

"No one is firing you, Lalita," said Nana. "Das is not himself today. Go home and come back tomorrow. You'll get your full wages for today. I believe in looking after everyone in Tolagunj, no matter who they are, as long as they follow rules and know their place."

Das took a step toward Lalita, fists clenched by his sides. He might have hit her if no one were around. He towered over her, glaring. I moved toward her and stopped.

Lalita was silhouetted against the dark sky and she was glowing, as if lit up from inside. Das's eyes widened, and then he spat on the ground and stomped away behind the haveli. I blinked, and she was back to her normal self. Had I imagined it? There was something strange about her, and I could deny it no longer. I looked at Nana to see if he had noticed anything, but he was looking at his watch impatiently.

Lalita pressed her head on the ground in front of Nana's feet, taking care to keep her distance. Every aspect of life was hard for Lalita, even something as simple as thanking someone. I made a mental note to remember this moment the next time I wanted to whine about something silly. My life was a breeze compared to Lalita's.

"Thank you, Sethji," said Lalita.

I was happy that Nana had listened to me. He had a kind heart even if he was eccentric and had a rogue for a servant, which didn't seem to bother him. *This incident should give me the ammo to convince him that Das is cruel and mad.* Nana went inside and shut the door. Lalita got to her feet wearily, wrapping her arms around her as a chill breeze gusted through the courtyard.

The air smelled metallic. The howling wind shook the treetops, as if to uproot them. Icy drops of rain pockmarked my face.

"I have to get home," said Lalita. "Thanks for speaking up for me."

"I can't let you walk home in a storm," I said. "It's not safe. Stay in here till the storm passes." I led the way to the cowshed, glancing back at the haveli's door and windows.

65

No one was looking out, and the kitchen was at the rear. The chances of Das seeing us were slim.

Dry leaves and dust danced ahead of us. The sky was midnight black. It was going to be a severe storm and Lalita would be safer waiting it out here. The shed was warm and smelled of milk and fresh grass. A couple of cows mooed softly when they saw us. A glowing lantern swung on a peg, throwing warm, buttery light through the shed.

I shut the door and bolted it. The cowshed had a bolt inside, I noted, but not my bedroom door. This confirmed my suspicion that Das was going to try something soon. Maybe even tonight when I was asleep. I had to be vigilant and catch him before he harmed me.

Inside the shed, the sound of the wind had lessened, and the cold wasn't as severe.

"As I was saying earlier today, before we got interrupted, I saw something odd in our kitchen today."

"Like what?" she said, flopping on a mound of hay and wiping the rain off her face. She looked hungry and exhausted.

"I think Das is, somehow, connected to the astrologer. The fraud astrologer makes these terrible predictions and then Das carries them out. He's evil—you saw that for yourself. He even threatened to kill me if I continued to ask questions and poke around. I think he's scared we'll discover his secret and then his game's up. I have to warn Nana before that madman harms him."

"What proof do you have that he's helping the astrologer?" said Lalita.

"The day wasps attacked me, I noticed that he'd been bitten too. That could only be if he'd been close to a nest. Also, with the fire in your fields—he could very easily have started it and then also helped put it out to remove suspicion from him. And I found a hidden door in the pantry, which is locked. The only one who uses the pantry is Das."

The wind whooshed through cracks in the shed as I recounted how the chicken feather had alerted me to the fact that the pantry was locked. Also, the hidden door at the end, and how Das had threatened me when he found me snooping around.

"But why?" said Lalita, frowning. "Das has a comfortable life looking after your grandfather. He has a roof over his head and three meals a day. It's more than what most of the villagers have. So much more than Ma and I could ever hope for."

"Maybe it's not enough," I replied. "Maybe he needs some danger and excitement in his life. To see how far he can go and still get away with it. Or maybe he's just mad."

Lalita stared at me. "There's only one person here with the over-the-top ideas, and it's not me."

It was my turn to frown. "Why is the cellar door in the pantry locked? Das tried to stop me. Why would he do this unless he was hiding something important? We have to get in there, find proof, and show it to Nana. That might convince him to get rid of Das. We might get rid of the astrologer and his dire predictions too."

The wind howled like a dog serenading the moon. A cold draft seeped in from under the door. Lalita shivered in her tattered clothes, and her face looked gray. She wrapped her threadbare dupatta over her arms and moved deeper into the cowshed.

I took off my sweater and held it out to her. "Here, take this. It'll keep you warm till the storm blows over."

She ran her fingers over the cloth. "So soft," she said. Then she slipped it on, hugged herself. "I've never had anything this nice! Can I keep it?"

It was my favorite sweater, but she needed it more than I did. "Sure."

"So, you want to explore the cellar?" she said, snuggling into the sweater. She'd stopped shivering and color was returning to her pinched face. "Why tell *me*? You live here, you can go any time."

"You are the bravest person I know," I said. "And smart. Please come with me." What I could not say, but truly believed, was that she was special. I refused to say "supernatural" because I didn't believe that, but something about Lalita had frightened Das.

A deep growl broke the silence. Lalita rubbed her belly. "I'm so hungry. You have anything to eat?"

"I'll be right back," I said.

Rain hurtled to the ground. The smell of wet earth filled the air. I slipped in through the front door, which was, thankfully, still unlocked. Voices from Nana's study meant Das was with him. I hurried to the kitchen and piled bread, cheese, a couple of samosas, and a ripe mango into a kitchen towel. I sneaked out the back door with my haul.

"This should keep you going until tonight," I said, handing the bundle to Lalita. "We'll explore the cellar when Nana and Das are asleep."

Lalita's face lit up momentarily at the sight of the food and then worry clouded her eyes again. "If I'm caught, I will be in a *lot* of trouble," she said.

"I can't do this without your help," I said. Having Lalita with me would help. I didn't know how or why; I just knew it would.

She lifted her chin and looked me in the eye. "You are kind, just like your grandmother," she said. "I'll do it. We'll go explore the cellar tonight."

14

I flopped down on the hay beside her, relieved that I wouldn't have to go to the cellar alone. Rain hammered the tin roof of the shed, but not a drop came in. I was reluctant to leave in this downpour and go to my cold, lonely room.

"Was Das always like this?" I asked. "When I last saw him, I was two, so obviously I don't remember a thing about him."

Lalita was chomping on the mango, skin and all, juice running down her chin. "He was strict but not cruel. He changed after your nani died last year. Your nani was a gem. She did not see me as an untouchable but as a person. I loved her." She wiped her lips with the back of her hand and gave me a shy smile. "This is so good. I've never eaten a mango that wasn't rotten."

My face was warm with shame. I'd always taken for granted that my next meal would appear whenever I wanted it and that it would be good and wholesome. Another thing Lalita had just made me realize.

"Nani and I talked on the phone often," I said. "She always asked me to visit, but my mother didn't want to come back here. She mentioned some fight she'd had with Nana. Now she wants to make it up to him, and here I am."

Lalita looked at me strangely. I knew what she was thinking. We'd stayed away for so long while Nani was alive. Now here we were, trying to get along with my grandfather, who was a stranger to us, and Nani was no more.

"Your nani was loved and respected in the village," said Lalita. "Even the adults were sobbing when she died of a heart attack. I miss her so much."

I missed Nani too. I'd enjoyed talking to her and if I closed my eyes, I could hear her soothing voice, even if I did not remember all the things we talked about. Often I felt she was still watching over me. Even her portrait's eyes had seemed to follow me when I had stepped into the haveli. I had told no one about it in case they said I had an overactive imagination.

"The villagers must love Nana, too, right?" I said. "He's kind and helpful."

Lalita's face hardened. "Sethji could do so much more, but he will not. He's cruel because of his indifference and his belief that we are still a caste to be hated. If he changed, the villagers would listen to him and change too. But that will probably never happen in Ma's or my lifetime." She swiped at the tear on her cheek.

"This is so unfair!" I said. "I'm going to talk to Nana once Mom and Dad are back. Maybe he'll listen to all of us and start treating you with more respect. The villagers will have to follow. First we have to get rid of Das."

A voice like a foghorn came from the haveli. "Lunch is ready, Avi Baba. Come now."

Talk of the devil. "I better go," I said. "Meet me in my room at midnight?"

Though Lalita looked worried, she nodded. I ran all the

way to the haveli and sneaked upstairs to change my T-shirt so no one would ask why I was soaking wet.

Nana joined us for lunch but was preoccupied. Once again, classical music played on the radio. The screechy music, the secluded haveli, the gloom, and the mystery of the astrologer and his predictions were getting me down. I couldn't wait to go back home.

"Food is missing from the kitchen," said Das, watching me closely. "Did you take it?"

"Come on, Das," said Nana irritably. "Avi is a growing boy. So what if he took some food without asking? This is his house, after all. Stop behaving like an old woman and serve lunch."

Das glowered at him. I threw Nana a grateful look, and he winked at me. It felt like we were bonding. Once I had evidence of Das's guilt, it would be easier to approach him. I might even get him to be kinder to Lalita so the villagers could do the same.

Lunch over, Nana announced he was taking a nap. It was too gloomy and dark to sit in my room and read. I decided to explore the house.

In the foyer, I stared up at Nani's portrait. Her kind eyes seemed to stare down at me. Her white hair shone like a halo.

"I wish I'd got to spend more time with you," I whispered. "Lalita says you were amazing."

Suddenly the portrait swayed, as if caught in a sudden gust of wind. I leaped back, barely holding back a scream. The window at the end of the corridor was shut tight. So where had the breeze come from? How had the portrait moved? As I straightened the portrait, I peeked behind it. Nothing but a solid wall. Just as my fingertips touched the frame, I felt a small jolt, as if I'd touched a live wire. I bolted from the corridor. There were no ghosts. It was all in my imagination.

I explored the rest of the house, taking care not to slip on the stairs, or step on loose floorboards. In more than one shabby room there was scrabbling in the wet, crumbling walls. *Rats.* The stink of ammonia hung in the air—probably rat poop. *This haveli must take a lot of money to maintain and even then it isn't enough, which is why it is falling to ruin.* I remembered seeing a section of it being overtaken by the forest when we'd first arrived. How was Nana surviving even though he was the zamindar? He should sell it and come to stay with us in Delhi. He'd be so much more comfortable, and we'd never have to come back to this place again. Chewing on how to broach the subject with Nana, I headed upstairs.

The moment I stepped into my room, I saw it. Propped up on my pillow was the head of a chicken. Lightning shimmied against the sky, illuminating its one eye that seemed to glare at me. I screamed.

No one came. Nana must have been asleep and this must be Das's idea of revenge for me taking food or some other silly reason. I forced myself to lift the chicken head and toss it out the window. I stripped off the pillowcase and threw it into the bathroom. This proved two things: I had not imagined that dead chicken, and Das was out to scare me. Why?

I sat down to plan my revenge. The cellar door from the pantry held the key. What would I find there? The longer I thought about it, the worse I felt. As if someone were twisting my guts.

Lalita was close by, and the thought comforted me. But what if Das caught us? She would be in a lot more trouble than me. Was it wrong of me to have asked her? But I'd asked, and she'd agreed. I desperately needed her help and support. No way could I handle this on my own.

At dinnertime, I tried to tune out the screechy music. It was impossible. I sighed deeply, wishing I could put on cheerful music to improve my mood.

"Can we please switch to another channel today?" I asked. "I'm sure Nani will still talk to us if we're listening to pop music." I knew I was being rude, but I was so sick of this music and Nana's old-fashioned beliefs. And anxiety about tonight was making me reckless.

"No," said Nana.

"Nana, I don't think ghosts can communicate with the living. It's all just superstition."

"You should not talk of things you know nothing about, Avi!" Nana snapped. "Please eat your food."

I sneaked a glance at Das, who was smirking. This man was making me more uneasy by the second. I had to talk to Nana and tell him what was on my mind. "Can I talk to you, privately, after we finish dinner?"

"Whatever you want to say, you can say in front of Das," said Nana sharply. "I trust Das with my life. I have no secrets from him."

But he has plenty from you.

"It's not important," I said. No way was I saying anything in front of Das. He would corner me the moment we were alone. I couldn't take that risk just yet.

Nana nodded. "In that case, goodnight." He switched off the radio carefully, his hands lingering over the knobs, caressing them. Now that I knew the reason he loved these radios, and played just the one channel, the whole thing took on a more sinister aspect. Had Nana lost touch with reality after Nani died? Was this the reason he couldn't see that Das was dangerous?

Das smiled at me as soon as Nana left the room. His eyes seemed to taunt me as he extracted the longest knife from the drawer and started to sharpen it, slowly, deliberately, his eyes riveted to mine.

I fled from the kitchen, pulse racing. I prayed I would survive till Mom and Dad came back.

15

_____

At midnight, Lalita knocked on my window and squeezed in. Even though I was wide awake and pacing the room, I startled as she dropped onto the floor. There was no moon tonight, and the darkness looked menacing. The rain had stopped, and the heat was a thick blanket, smothering us. Frogs croaked in the pond, loud and insistent. Crickets chirped. The house was deathly silent.

"Let's go," I said, my stomach gurgling with anxiety. "The sooner we get this over with, the better."

"Avi," she said, clutching my sleeve, "if Sethji or Das catch me inside the house, they'll punish me. The panchayat is looking for any excuse to throw Ma and me out of Tolagunj." Her voice shook. "I'm not sure I should do this."

I stared at her. On the one hand, I didn't want her to get into any more trouble. On the other, I had to solve this mystery once and for all. Not knowing was worse than facing whatever it was in the cellar.

"We have to get to the bottom of this if we want to stop Das from destroying any more property or harming animals," I said. "If he was responsible for the fire at your place, the panchayat will punish him instead of you. I also think he had something to do with the wasps. I told you about the bite marks on his arms, right? He's guilty and we just have to find proof. I know we will find it in the cellar he's guarding."

Lalita wiped the sweat off her face and took a deep, ragged breath.

"If you end up having to leave the village, you can have my cell phone and all the pocket money I have," I said. "It's the latest model and will get you a good price if you sell it." At least she wouldn't be penniless.

Lalita gave a bitter laugh. "You are clueless, aren't you? You seriously think a cell phone and a few rupees will make up for me losing my home?"

My face burned as I realized what a huge mistake I'd made. I had to think before I spoke and put myself in her shoes before I tried to "help".

"I'm sorry, Lalita. I'm being selfish. Go back home. I'll handle this alone." It cost me every ounce of my willpower not to beg her to come with me. But this had to be her decision. I could not, would not, guilt her into doing something that could have dire consequences.

"I'll go with you," said Lalita. "I want to find out who destroyed our field too. If it was deliberate, I want the person caught and punished."

Relief flooded me, and her bravery gave me courage. "Let's do this."

The door creaked as I opened it, and I winced. "We're going down the stairs and into the kitchen," I said. "The pantry is beside the back door. Follow me."

We crept down the stairs and sat on the last step for a

few minutes while our eyes adjusted. I didn't want to bump into anything and wake up Nana or Das.

The kitchen was deserted. A faint smell of curry lingered in the air. The tap in the sink dripped steadily. Thunder boomed overhead and died away.

I pulled open the pantry door, which was unlocked. The fragrance of ripening mangoes wafted out—it was the smell of summer holidays, of sunshine, and picnics. But it felt wrong coming from a pantry in a crumbling haveli that held sinister secrets.

"Can I take one for my mother?" Lalita asked, jerking her chin at the basket.

"Help yourself," I said, trying not to sound irritated. I reminded myself that they could not afford these luxuries, and she was only looking out for her family.

She slipped one into her pocket. "Ma will be so happy," she murmured. "Thanks!"

"Careful not to knock anything over," I said, remembering the crash when the pickle jar had fallen. The slightest sound would bring Das running. Nana too. My heartbeat was so loud in my ears I was sure they'd hear it if they were awake.

There was no sliver of light at the back of the pantry. Was it just a storage space, as Das had said? Was I risking Lalita's future and safety for nothing?

I shut the pantry door and switched on the light. A thick blanket lay folded against the bottom of the door to the cellar. *This* was why no light showed up. I pulled out my flashlight and kicked the blanket aside.

"We're going down," I said, turning off the light.

The heat was stifling in here, and I was already feeling trapped. I turned the handle, and the door swung open. A flight of stone steps curved away from us into darkness. I turned on my flashlight, my pulse thundering in my ears. Did I dare face my death? I shook my head. It was all a nonsense, and I was going to prove it. The villagers, and Nana, would thank Lalita and me.

We shuffled down the steps, the flashlight illuminating the way. The air down here was cool and musty. After a couple of steep turns, I heard soft classical music. Who was playing music in the cellar?

"Still want to go on?" I asked, hoping Lalita would talk me out of this dangerous mission.

"We've come this far," she whispered. "Let's see it through."

"What if Das catches us?" I whispered.

"Even if he does, you'll only get a scolding," she said.

What she didn't say was that *she* wasn't safe. My respect for her climbed another notch. I had to protect her in any way I could.

"Let me go first," I said. "If I see anything weird, I'll raise the alarm. Run before you get caught. Promise?"

Lalita nodded. "Promise."

I took a deep breath and before I could lose my nerve, I hurried down the steps and eased the door open a crack.

I gaped, unable to believe my eyes.

16

I was in a well-lit room with shelves covering every inch of wall space. Each shelf had an assortment of radios. Some were antiques with old-fashioned dials, and some were very new. This explained how and why the radios in the kitchen changed daily. About twenty radios were on, playing the same classical music channel that Nani loved.

Nana sat in a chair in the center of the room, eyes closed, fingers steepled in utter concentration. Was he seriously expecting Nani to talk to him? Suddenly all the radios went silent and then started up again, as if they'd hiccupped. Goosebumps erupted all over my skin. I'd landed up in a haveli of horrors.

"Go back up," I mouthed to Lalita, jerking a thumb upward. I wanted to get out of here before Nana noticed us and started asking questions. And if Nana was here, Das wouldn't be far off. I eased the door shut and shuffled backward as fast as I could, and ran into a warm brick wall. We yelped and whirled around. Das glared at us, arms crossed across his massive chest.

"Snooping on your grandfather, Avi Baba?" His gaze

flicked to Lalita, and his expression turned ugly. "No untouchable has *ever* defiled this house. How dare you step inside?"

"Stop yelling at her," I said, shielding her from Das. "I asked her to come with me. If you have to yell at anyone, it's me."

Das herded us down the steps to where Nana stood at the open door. The radios were silent. "Even if you're unable to understand or follow customs and traditions, Lalita, you should know better than to step inside. This will not go unpunished."

Lalita whimpered. "I'm sorry," she said in a shaky voice. "I only wanted to help Avi."

I was so angry a red film seemed to have covered my eyes, tinting the room crimson. "I told you, she did nothing except listen to me," I said.

Das's eyes flicked over Lalita. "Turn out your pockets."

She turned white, and I remembered, too late, the mango she had taken for her mother. She stood still, gaping at them both.

"Pay attention, girl!" said Nana, snapping his fingers in front of her face. "Das doesn't like to repeat instructions."

Lalita held out the mango in a trembling hand.

Das snatched it from her and pocketed it.

"Stealing is a crime," said Nana. "I will have to confiscate your land as punishment for trespassing on my property. You and your mother must leave Tolagunj. We cannot allow thieves to live here. Get out of this house and tell Shanti to pack up."

"NO!" I yelled. "This is too harsh a punishment for a single mango, which I *gave* her. Punish me instead."

"Let it go, Avi," said Lalita. "This is an excuse to throw us out. If this does not work, they will keep trying until we leave. We might as well go now." She sprinted out of the basement, sobbing.

"You're both bullies," I said, glaring at Nana. My throat was tight. I wanted to smash something. Maybe one of those expensive radios.

"And you're disobedient," said Nana, his eyes cold.

"Can you not forgive her this once?" I pleaded. "If you do that, I'll do whatever you say and stay in my room until Mom and Dad get back. That's a promise."

"Too late for that now," said Nana, dismissing me with a wave of his hand. "I'll talk to the panchayat about Lalita before the fair on Sunday and let them know my recommendation. You may attend the fair with Das, but you are *not* to leave the house before that. You are in the ground."

Das poked me in the back to make me go faster. I wanted to whip around and knock him down the stairs.

Even though I knew it would get me buried for real, I couldn't help yelling at Nana, "The word is 'grounded', and only my parents can do that, you big bully! Nani would never have been so unfair, nor would she have let you behave this way. I wish she were still here!"

Suddenly static filled the cellar, loud and crackly. It was as if all the radios had turned on.

Nana's face was white, and my pulse raced. Had Nani heard me?

17

The next day was torture. Das had locked me in my room and brought my meals up to me. I tried to climb out of the window to run to the village with my cell phone and call Mom. Unfortunately, one vine snapped under me and I screamed in panic. Das heard me and waited till I got on the ground before marching me back to my room.

"Nana!" I yelled. There was no answer.

"Save your breath," said Das. "Nana is not here. He has gone to the next village on business. I convinced him I would look after you very well."

His tone, more than anything else, made my heart shiver. I'd better behave or I would not survive till Sunday. Had it only been a few days since I had arrived at the haveli? It seemed like years had passed.

Rain lashed the house and seeped in through swollen windowpanes. The phone lines were sure to be down, so there was no word from Mom and Dad. None from Lalita, either. I spent most of my time by the window, staring out at the sodden landscape, wondering how she was, what had happened to her. I hoped she was all right.

I did nothing to antagonize Das all the next day, and he allowed me to have my dinner in the kitchen that evening. Nana was still not back, and I wondered if Das had murdered him and hidden his body in the cellar. My imagination was going wild. If I ever survived this ordeal, Mom and Dad were both going to get an earful of this, and I'd never let them forget how they'd abandoned me to these weirdos. I was a prisoner, make no mistake. There was no point trying to sneak into Nana's office to call Mom or Dad on the landline. I would likely not get through and Das would only get meaner.

I bided my time.

A patch of brilliant blue sky greeted me on Sunday morning. After three days of being cooped up in the haveli, I couldn't wait to get out. Mom and Dad were coming back today, and I was going to the fair, where I would see the astrologer and settle my death forecast once and for all. I also planned to keep an eye on Das and maybe catch him in the act of colluding with the astrologer.

I flung off the bedsheet and jumped out of bed with new resolve. I'd tell Lalita how sorry I was for getting her into trouble, and buy her the sweets I had promised. I would also talk to Mr. Venkat and convince him not to punish her, since this was all my fault.

Nana had been the biggest disappointment of all: kindly, naive, and spineless. Unfair, too, for punishing Lalita for a single mango.

In the kitchen, Das slurped tea from a large mug and looked at me as he would a pariah dog.

"Where is Nana?" I asked, taking my usual seat. It was good to be out of my room again. I was itching to feel the sunlight on my face and breathe in a lungful of fresh air.

"How many parathas?" said Das.

83

He'd become increasingly rude and obnoxious whenever we were alone. I couldn't wait to catch him out. If anyone needed a lesson in humility, it was him. But he also scared me. Until Mom and Dad arrived, I'd have to watch my step.

"Two," I said, being equally brief and rude.

Das poured a mug of tea from a pot simmering on the stove and plunked it in front of me. Ginger cardamom–flavored steam perfumed the air. I took a sip as I made plans for the day. The first thing was to get to the fair and find Lalita. Once I knew she was okay, I'd figure out a way to expose that fraud astrologer.

"I have to call Mom," I said.

"Phone is still dead," said Das, not bothering to turn around as he made my breakfast.

I made a mental note to find one in the village and was by the front door in record time. There was lots to do today and not a minute to lose.

The village was bustling, and the air smelled fresh after the downpour. I scanned the crowds for Lalita. My eyes were peeled for Venkat too, so I could talk to him before the panchayat passed judgement and threw her and her mother out of the village. I only hoped I wasn't too late.

"There's Venkat," I said, pointing. "But where is Nana? I have to talk to them both about Lalita."

"Around someplace, taking care of important business," said Das. "You are not to disturb either of them. No one will believe you anyway, so don't waste your breath. I have some things to take care of. I'll be back in a couple of hours."

This was it. Das was getting ready to meet the astrologer or else he'd never let me out of his sight. All I needed to do was find the astrologer's tent and look out for Das, who was sure to be around, listening to the predictions to carry them out later.

As the sun climbed high in the sky, the sherbet vendors did roaring business. Food smells filled the air, and the cacophony grew as various rides filled up. A long line snaked out from an open tent at the center of the fair. The astrologer was here.

I walked toward the front of the line, making sure there were lots of people between me and the astrologer. I wanted to eavesdrop before I made my presence known.

This time the astrologer was suspended a few feet off the ground, a saffron robe draped around him. Even though I knew it was a trick, he looked impressive, floating in the air. Villagers chatted and jostled, awaiting their turn. As before, a curtain of beads covered the astrologer's face. They clinked softly as he talked.

"Make sure to donate one sack of grain *each* to the temple and to the zamindar," the astrologer said in a somber yet booming voice, "or your family will starve the rest of the year."

I was so sick of the constant bad news, the doom and gloom of his predictions, I could contain myself no longer. I stomped out from behind the villagers and raced to the front of the line.

"If you listen to this fraud, your family will starve," I said, glaring at the astrologer. "Ignore him."

An unshaven villager with a lazy eye stared at me open-mouthed.

"I see you're still in good health," said the astrologer. "Not for long."

He reeked of sweat and the same sickly-sweet incense that made me want to gag. His eyes, behind the beads, glittered.

85

"You're nothing but a fraud!" I said. "Where is your assistant who carries out the *predictions* that you make? And who are you? Where do you come from?"

"Pay attention," the astrologer said, snapping his fingers in front of my face. "Today you will die, unless you spend the entire day in your room, reciting prayers!"

I stood still, as if entombed in ice. It wasn't the warning that had paralyzed me. It was the *way* he'd said it.

Finally, I had guessed the true identity of the astrologer.

18

I took a step toward him. "You're—"

Das lunged forward and clapped a hand on my mouth. With a muffled cry, I twisted and fought. It was like wrestling with a bear. Das dragged me away from the astrologer's tent, his hand still over my mouth.

"Give way, please," said Das, cleaving a path through the villagers. "Move aside, this boy is going to be sick."

The villagers moved aside, giving us curious glances.

"Help!" I yelled. "He's kidnapping me!"

But with Das's hand over my mouth, it came out all garbled. No one came forward to rescue me, and within minutes we'd left the fair behind and were on the outskirts of the village. Das took his hand away but kept a firm grip on my arm. It felt like a steel clamp.

"Why did you pull me away?" I yelled. "I wanted to talk to him."

"Did you not see that line of paying customers?" said Das. "Everyone has to earn a living."

"I want to go back," I said. Surely I had been mistaken

about his identity. My brain was short-circuiting with what I had just figured out.

"Where is Nana?" I asked. "I need to talk to him right now."

"Did I not tell you he's busy in the next village? He will be back this evening."

"You're lying!" I snapped, wrenching my arm away from him. "He's right here and we both know it."

Das shrugged, supremely unconcerned.

"I have to find Lalita," I said.

"We are going back to the haveli and you will stay in your room," said Das. "After all, *I* believe in the astrologer and we have to keep you safe."

"No!" I said. But I was wasting my breath. This gorilla was ten times my size. I had no choice but to follow him.

Back at the haveli, I paced around the house. I tried to get into Nana's study to use the phone, but the door was locked. So was the front door. Das had chopped down all the vines around my bedroom window so there was no escaping from there, either.

I went to the foyer and gazed at Nani's portrait. She made me feel a little calmer, although I was a prisoner in this haveli.

"Wish you were here, Nani. Either I'm going mad or the people in this house are. I need help but I don't know where to go."

I said all this in a whisper. Somehow, speaking to a dead person's portrait felt strange. But there was no one else I could talk to, and I was desperate. If only I'd looked for Lalita first, instead of that weird astrologer, we could have figured this out together. Where was she? I was really worried about her safety.

The surface of the portrait rippled. I glanced at the

window. It was shut. *Was* the haveli haunted? All the evidence was there, yet...

The day crawled by so slowly, watching a pot of water boil might have been exciting. Evening brought the sounds of crickets and frogs, but no Nana. Mom and Dad weren't here either. Could Das be telling the truth? Was Nana really visiting the neighboring village? But I knew what I saw and heard in the astrologer's tent. My head was a jumble of thoughts. I missed Lee and Lalita. Most of all, I missed normal.

Das made me sit in the kitchen while he prepared the evening meal.

"When is Nana coming back?" I asked for the umpteenth time.

"He'll come when he comes," said Das. "You are not to wait up for him."

"Where is Lalita?"

"She's too ashamed to show her face in the village after what she did," said Das. "No more questions."

I ate dinner while Das eyed me like a vulture watching a dying animal. As soon as I was done, he whisked my plate away and ordered me upstairs.

Back in my room, I climbed into bed, fully dressed. There was no way I'd get any sleep. It was just after nine in the evening, and I had a feeling Das would be along to check on me. I was right. Ten minutes after I'd climbed into bed, he crept into my room and stood over me, breathing heavily.

It took all my willpower to stay still and breathe evenly. After what must have been barely a minute but felt like an hour, he left, shutting the door softly behind him.

I forced myself to wait fifteen minutes before I got out of bed. I tiptoed to the door and put my ear to it. There was no sound. There was something weird going on tonight, and I was going to find out what it was. With any luck, Mom and Dad would be here soon, and I could share my information with them. And then insist we leave.

I tied a couple of bedsheets together, secured them to the legs of the bed, and threw them out the window. Das thought that by cutting the vines he could stop me. He was mistaken.

Scared as I was, I inched my way down the bedsheets, and after a few agonizing minutes, I stood on the ground. I made my way to the back of the house, keeping to the shadows. The air was sultry and still. Even the night sounds were muted, as if every creature was just too exhausted to make a sound.

The lights in the kitchen were off. Some distance away, Das was chopping wood by the light of a lantern. The thwack of the axe each time it split the wood made me cringe. Hopefully, it would keep him occupied long enough for me to make a dash to the cellar and back up again. That place held the key to the puzzle, and I was going to find it. Today.

I tiptoed into the house using the back door, and raced into the pantry. My mouth was dry, and my breath came in short, sharp bursts, as if I'd run a 10K marathon. Luckily, the door to the cellar was also unlocked. Das hadn't expected me to get out of my locked room and he wasn't being careful.

I stepped into the room of radios and flicked the light on. The silence was worse than the music. The radios, about fifty of them, gleamed and winked at me.

The room smelled like Nana and I looked around nervously, almost expecting him to pop out of a corner. A heart-pounding minute raced by with no one appearing. I forced myself to walk around the room, knocking on the walls. I worked carefully, convinced there was something here that I was missing.

Opposite the door I'd entered was a section that sounded hollow. My hunch had been right.

I rapped again, my heart thudding in tandem against my ribcage. "Anyone in there?" I said, moving aside the radios and putting my ear to the wall.

"Help!" said a voice I recognized well.

19

"Lalita!" I said, relief and fear washing over me. "Can you tell me how to get in?"

Her muffled voice called out instructions that I could barely hear, but I refused to give up. Again, following my instincts and with a bit of luck, I found the lever, cleverly hidden under a shelf. I pulled and a section of the wall hinged outward, revealing a narrow doorway.

A coppery stink oozed out of the shadowy room. I forced myself to step inside. A low-watt bulb hanging from a grimy wire illuminated Lalita, tied up in a chair. A rivulet of dried blood ran down one side of her face, which was streaked with tears.

"Are you okay?" I said, racing over to her. "Who did this to you?"

Her head lolled. "Water," she gasped.

I remembered the glass I'd seen beside Nana's chair. Grabbing it, I raced back to Lalita. I held the glass to her lips while she gulped greedily.

"Thank you."

"How long have you been here?" I asked, trying not to gag at the sight of the blood, at the sight of her gray face.

"Since last night," she said faintly. "Das kidnapped me . . . dragged me here . . . side entrance." She breathed raggedly, her face becoming even grayer.

"Come on, let's get you out of here," I said, tugging at the rope on her wrists with shaking hands. I'd race to the village for help the moment we were safely outside. I hoped Mom and Dad would arrive and save me the trip, but there was no sound of an approaching car. We were on our own with Das and Nana.

At last, Lalita was free. She slid to the floor and lay still. I forced her to sit up and shook her gently. "Lalita, wake up so we can get out of here. I can't carry you."

"She's going nowhere, and neither are you," said an icy voice.

I whipped around and felt a cool breeze on my face. Das and the astrologer stood beside a door beyond which was darkness. So, this is how they got in and out without going through the house. Clever.

"Let us go or I'm calling the police," I said, trying to sound confident despite the tremble in my voice. We were so dead.

Das laughed. "The police are in Sethji's pocket. They will not touch his loyal servant."

Lalita moaned softly, leaning against the wall.

"I predict she will not last the night," said the astrologer. "Sorry, Avi."

"Shut up!" I yelled as I grabbed the astrologer's turban and pulled it off. The words stuck in my throat as I saw his face properly for the first time.

"Oh, Avi, now look what you've done," said Nana, an evil grin across his face.

"I guessed it was you," I said, taking a step back. My hunch in the market had been correct, even though my brain had refused to believe it had been Nana. "This was how you knew I was an only child and allergic to wasps."

Nana stared at me, his black eyes not leaving my face.

I crouched beside Lalita, trying to help her stand. "And you helped carry out Nana's *warnings*," I said, glaring at Das.

"Aren't you a clever boy!" said Das. But he wasn't smiling.

What a fool I'd been. This was why Nana had no secrets from Das. They were *both* in on this astrologer scheme.

"Why?" I asked, wanting to keep them talking till Mom and Dad got here. It was our best chance of staying alive. "Why are you doing all this?"

"Because I have a kind heart," said Nana. "Come, let us get comfortable and I'll explain."

They marched me back into the radio room. Das carried Lalita and dumped her beside me. Nana sank into his armchair with a sigh. "What would you like to know, Avi?"

"Why are you terrorizing your own villagers?" I asked.

"A zamindar has many expenses," he said with a deep sigh. "So many that I am *always* short of cash to keep this haveli in repair. The government is raising taxes every year, so I have to get creative with ways of earning income. Sometimes, I just want a piece of land for myself. But I always warn the person in advance and give them a chance to do the right thing. Don't I, Das?"

"Yes, Sethji." Das stood with his hands behind his back, nodding.

"You're a cruel and terrible person," I said. "Das is no better. He set the wasps on me and switched my EpiPen. I could have died."

Das nodded. "We only wanted to scare you. I had the EpiPen with me. I would have given you a dose if you were really in danger. But Lalita poked her nose and spoiled the plan."

"But why?" I said to Nana. "I'm family. How could you think of harming your own grandson?"

"It's *because* of that reason," said Nana. "I did not want you or anyone interfering with my setup. We tried to keep you in your room, Das and I, but you did not take the hint."

I remembered the locked door on the very first night. Das must have locked me in and quietly unlocked it the next morning. It wasn't the damp that made the door stick. It was Das.

"If you found out what was going on, you'd tell Aruna and she would force me to go live with her or, worse, put me in a home or institution. No, I prefer my independence and getting what I want *when* I want it. I am the zamindar of Tolagunj, after all. And after Das got rid of Venkat's cow, he's deeply in debt to me. Even if I'm caught, he will do precisely as I say or lose everything."

It all made sense now. That agile intruder had been Das. I also remembered that Nana had asked Venkat for collateral on the loan. That must have been his house or something equally valuable. Nana had planned this out well and it would have worked, if not for me.

"You're sick in the head," I said. "You need help. Both of you."

"I warned Shanti and Lalita to give up the land," Nana continued, as if I hadn't spoken at all. "Untouchables have no right to own property. They would have let it go to waste. If they had willingly given it to me, I would have let them stay on as caretakers. But no—"

Lalita sat up just then, her eyes dark with hate. "You've been after our land for months and you predicted something bad would happen if we didn't hand it over to you.

When Ma refused, you had Das burn our crops. You're *worse* than all the terrible things you accuse us of being. You're Death itself. And I knew that."

Nana eyed her coldly. "I did not give you permission to speak in my house. I'll have to spend a lot of money to purify this place once again. And I'll have to find a permanent solution to keeping you and your mother quiet. You too, Avi! You know too much."

My mouth was so dry I could barely swallow. "If Nani were still alive, she would never let you get away with this."

His cruel gaze convinced me he was greedy enough to do exactly that, even though I was family. They could have easily killed Lalita and disposed of her body if I hadn't found her when I did. Who but her mother would care about her going missing? And now I was going to die too. I made one more attempt to appeal to him.

"Lalita and I both promise not to tell anyone. Can we go, please, Nana?"

"It's too late," he said.

"No, it's not," said Lalita. "Sethaniji always helped me out and she will do so again."

Oh, no, Lalita, not you too. Not now. I hoped she wasn't losing her mind when a sudden chill swept through the room, making me shiver. Someone whispered my name, but it had to be my imagination. Nani was dead, and there was no way she could help.

"I have to take care of something and I'll be back soon," said Nana.

"Wait!" I yelled. "Lalita is hurt and needs help. At least let *her* go back home." If I could get her to safety, I'd figure out a plan for myself. She was in this mess because of me, and the guilt made me sick. "If anything happens to her, I promise you, I will talk to the police in the city and make sure you both end up in jail!"

"Das, tie them up."

Struggling against Das was a waste of energy, so I didn't even try. *Better to conserve it for our escape.* Within minutes, he'd tied Lalita and me back to back. The rope bit into my skin every time I moved. Lalita shook with silent sobs.

This was it. Unless we came up with a plan, we were both going to die.

The astrologer's predictions would come true, after all.

20

"Lalita, are you okay?"

Lalita did not move. She must have passed out again.

I still couldn't believe what Nana had done. Had Nani's death driven him to insanity, or did he always have an evil, greedy streak, which had surfaced now that there was no one to keep him in check?

An hour passed, then two. I squirmed hard, my numb fingertips grazing over the rope. It bit into my skin until it was raw. My hands were slick with my own blood. I stopped. Something dark scurried in a corner. Rats!

"HELP!" I yelled. "Mom, Dad, Nani—please help!"

I stopped. I don't even know why that last one slipped out. Nani was dead. Why would I call for a dead person?

Lalita twitched.

"Lalita!" I said, twisting around. "Are you okay?"

"Yes," she said, faintly.

"Can you move your hands?" I yelled. "We've got to loosen the knots before the rats get to us."

We scooched closer and tugged at the ropes. It was no use. The knots were tight, and we were too weak.

My wrists were bleeding. Lalita shivered beside me, pale and weak. She'd been without food for a longer time. I didn't know how much longer her strength would last.

"Lalita, you said that my nani always looked out for you. Maybe if we both call out to her, she might listen." I felt like a fool saying this, especially when, until now, I'd not believed in the supernatural. I was desperate and willing to grab any straw.

"Sethaniji," said Lalita, her voice so weak it was almost inaudible.

Believe, I told myself. "Nani, we need you, please!"

Suddenly Lalita shuddered and cried out as the room filled with a dank, rotten smell. There was that chill again, as if someone had left the refrigerator door open.

"Lalita, are you okay?"

The ropes around our wrists suddenly snapped. I was free. I scrambled to my feet and turned to help Lalita. She was already on her feet, massaging her wrists and looking around. Despite the cut on her forehead, she looked strong and furious.

She smiled at me. It was totally unlike her usual shy smile. "You don't sound your usual self."

Lalita laughed hysterically.

"Stop it!" I said. "You're sounding scary."

"Try angry," she said. "Wouldn't *you* be if you had been treated like garbage all your life?" she added bitterly. "Two birds with one stone today."

She sounded so unlike the Lalita I knew, she was scaring me. I backed away a little, watching her. I hoped the stress hadn't made her snap.

A door slammed overhead. Footsteps thumped down the stairs.

"They're coming back," I said, trying not to sound desperate. "And we don't even have a plan."

"Relax," she said, standing tall. "Let me handle this."

Her eyes glowed silver and there was a calmness about her that hadn't been there before. She looked like she had that time in the courtyard when Das was about to yell at her. Somehow, I knew it was going to be all right. I had probably known it all along, which is why I had believed in Lalita and begged for her help.

Das stomped into the radio room. He must have noticed we weren't there and raced into the smaller one. He snarled when he saw us. "How did you untie yourselves? What trickery is this?"

He lunged for Lalita first, but she sidestepped him neatly and raised her arm. Das flew back and slammed into a wall.

His agonized yell reverberated in the small room.

21

Lalita stood quietly, humming a tune, while Das struggled to get to his feet.

Nana burst into the room just then. "What is going on, Das? What are you doing on the floor?"

He noticed that Lalita and I were both free. He lunged at her, but with a flick of her hand, Lalita stopped him cold. Then she pushed her palm forward. Nana slid backward, tripped on Das, and fell over.

"How dare you raise a hand to your wife, Ballu?" Lalita said in a commanding voice. "Shame on you."

"Na-nani?" I said in a whisper. "You're here?"

Lalita slowly turned her head and looked at me. Her silver eyes seemed to bathe me in a warm light. "Yes, Avi. You called for help and I *had* to answer. This madness has gone far enough."

Nana's face resembled old newspaper. He sat up, clutching his knees to his chest like a scared little boy. "This can't be," he muttered over and over. "You kids are playing games. Stop it, now!"

The cold was so intense now, I shivered and hugged myself. The stench of decay made it hard to breathe.

Lalita strolled over to Nana and crouched down. "How does it feel to be scared and helpless, Ballu? Are you enjoying being terrified just the way you scare the poor villagers?" "It can't be . . . this is impossible," he said. "Uma, is that really you?"

"Don't you recognize me, Ballu?" Nani-in-Lalita stretched out a hand and caressed Nana's cheek. Something dropped onto the floor from beneath black fingernails. An earthworm. She lifted it and popped it into her mouth. I tried not to gag.

"Don't you dare touch Sethji," said Das.

Lalita looked up at him calmly. She clenched her hand into a fist. Das clutched his chest and gasped, as if he were having a heart attack.

"Stop!" he moaned.

Nani-in-Lalita loosened her fist and Das keeled over, whimpering. She came over to me. "You've grown, Avi. And I'm so proud of you. You did not follow the outdated customs and traditions in Tolagunj. You befriended Lalita and treated her with respect. Therefore, I decided to help when you both called out to me."

It was so odd to see Lalita standing in front of me but hear Nani's familiar and calm voice. "It was the right thing to do," I said softly. "Lalita is a person, just like me. No one should be treated the way she is around here. But I have a question, Nani—why did you possess Lalita? Why not me? I'm your grandson, after all."

Nani-in-Lalita smiled. "Because her spirit is stronger than all of you put together." She glanced at Nana. "Being possessed by a ghost could kill a normal being. Not Lalita.

She has more courage than anyone I know, and she believes in the spirit world. Always has."

Nani-in-Lalita walked back to Nana. "I'm watching you, Ballu. One more toe out of line and *I* predict you will lose every bit of land you own. You'll be a beggar in your own village. You have sucked the blood of these villagers long enough."

Nana whimpered. "I'll be good, Uma. I switched on the radios every day. Why did you not speak to me?"

"The evil in your heart kept me away," said Nani-in-Lalita. "It was terrible to watch you become more cruel, day after day, while pretending to be kind. You will return *all* the land and livestock you usurped through your *predictions*, including Lalita's. Was it on your orders that it was set on fire?"

"Yes," said Nana softly. "It is a prime piece of land. I wanted it."

"You're a thief and a coward," said Nani-in-Lalita.

"Wait till I get my hands on you," said Das, struggling to his feet. "How dare you insult Sethji!"

Nani-in-Lalita clenched her fist again, and Das groaned and passed out. Or died. I really didn't care. After the way he'd tortured us, he deserved all the pain and suffering and more.

Nana looked up. "Let me keep *some* land, Uma. I still need to maintain this house."

Nani-in-Lalita glared at him. A laser beam of silver hit his forehead. He howled in pain as the spot scorched. "I'll do as you say, Uma. Forgive me."

"You have more sense than both these oafs put together, Avi," Nani said. "Keep an eye on them for me and forgive this foolish and greedy man. He was not always like this. Tell your mother, my sweet Aruna, to forgive him."

I nodded. "Yes, Nani, and thank you!"

Nani-in-Lalita came over to me. My heart thudded. She reached out a hand and stroked my hair. "I will always watch over you." Her eyes had that sweet, kind look I remembered.

Nani-in-Lalita sank to her knees. The stench disappeared, and so did the chill. The room was suddenly hot and stuffy.

Lalita dry-heaved, trembling violently. "I blacked out," she said. "What happened?" Her eyes fell on Das, then Nana. She shrank away, and I knew my Lalita was back.

I hugged her tight. "You're all right and that's all that matters."

Footsteps pounded down the stairs. Mom and Dad burst into the room.

"We knocked, but no one answered," she said, flinging her arms around me. "We searched the house from top to bottom and found the pantry door open. What's going on?"

We all stared at Nana. I wondered what lie he was going to spin. He got to his feet, slowly, painfully. "It's a long story. I've been a fool, but it's time to mend my ways. Let's all go up and I'll explain everything."

We settled down around the dining table while Das hobbled around making tea, rubbing his head where he'd slammed into the wall. His arrogance was gone, and he seemed deflated and scared. About time.

Lalita touched my shoulder. "I better get back home. Ma must be worried about me."

"Thank you for everything," I said. "I'll come see you tomorrow and bring over my allowance money as promised." This time neither Nana nor Das said anything. They knew better than to bring up the untouchable angle again.

As she hurried toward the door, Nana loomed in front of her. She stopped, looking like a cornered deer. Her frightened eyes darted between me and the back door.

"Please let her go, Nana," I said.

Nana sank to his knees and reached out for Lalita's hand. He clasped it in both of his. "I have wronged you and for that I am deeply sorry. I would like you to stay and have tea with us and hear what I have to say. You have played a very important part in it even if you can't remember what happened. After we've finished, we will go meet your mother together. I owe her an apology too. Of all the people, my beloved Uma chose *you* to communicate with me. After today, neither I nor anyone else will mistreat you—or they will be evicted. As of this moment, the word 'untouchable' is banned. You have the word of the zamindar of Tolagunj."

Mom's mouth fell open. Dad looked bewildered. Das swore under his breath. I smiled when I met Lalita's eyes. She smiled back.

Thanks, Nani, you're awesome.

IF YOU ENJOYED THIS BOOK, please join my mailing list at www.mahtabnarsimhan.com/newsletter for book news, giveaways, exclusive content, reading recommendations, and a favorite recipe!

BEFORE YOU GO, please review the book on Amazon.

It would be most appreciated, and your review will help me get the books in the hands of more readers who might also enjoy this story.

Thank you!

AUTHOR'S NOTE

The caste system in India, which divides Hindus into rigid social groups based on their work (karma) or their duty (dharma, which also stands for religion), is over 3000 years old.

An important and authoritative text on Hindu law called the Manusmriti "acknowledges and justifies the caste system as the basis of order and regularity of society."

The caste system has four major categories: Brahmins (priests and teachers), Kshatriyas (warriors and rulers), Vaishyas (farmers, traders, merchants), and Shudras (labourers). Outside of this class structure are the Dalits (untouchables or *achoots*.) There are multiple sub-divisions within each caste.

Many people believe these groups originated from Brahma, the god of creation. It is also believed that the Brahmins came from Brahma's head, the Kshatriyas came from his arms, the Vaishyas came from his thighs, and the Shudras from his feet.

The caste system influences almost every aspect of social and religious interaction within communities, with the upper castes repressing members of the lower castes. Even in the recent past, inter-marriage between castes was not allowed and was punishable by death. Very restrictive and unjust, it has prevailed for centuries, trapping people in a system from which there is no escape.

However, some Dalits like BR Ambedkar and KR Narayanan have broken free of the caste system to hold prestigious positions in India, paving the way for other members of excluded groups.

Source: https://www.bbc.com/news/world-asia-india-35650616
Recommended for further reading:
Bhimrao Ambedkar: The Boy Who Asked Why
Turning the Pot, Tilling the Land: Dignity of Labour in Our Times
Savitribai Phule and I
Bhimayana: Experiences of Untouchability (Kindle)
Bhimayana: Experiences of Untouchability (Hardcover/Paperback)
Year of the Weeds
On Mythology: Mythopedia: An Encyclopedia of Mythical Beasts and Their Magical Tales by Good Wives and Warriors

ABOUT THE AUTHOR

Mahtab Narsimhan has had four careers in her lifetime. Writing is her fifth and favorite. She has worked in the hotel industry, the credit card industry, as well as the recruitment industry (general and IT).

Mahtab immigrated to Canada in 1997 and started writing in 2004. Her debut novel, *The Third Eye*, won the Silver Birch Fiction Award in 2009 and she hasn't looked back since. Mahtab is deeply committed to representing diversity in her stories. For more information, please visit her website at www.mahtabnarsimhan.com

More Books by Mahtab Narsimhan
(Available anywhere books are sold. Please see her website for more information.)
The Tiffin
Mission Mumbai (Teachers' Pick)
Embrace the Chicken
Genie Meanie
Valley of the Rats
Project Bollywood (April 2022)
Careful What You Wish For (Aug 2022)

Picture Books:
Looking for Lord Ganesh
You and Me Both

facebook.com/MahtabNarsimhanWriter

twitter.com/MahtabNarsimhan

instagram.com/mahtab_narsimhan

ACKNOWLEDGMENTS

Thank you to my wonderful friends and writers, Amber Cowie, Diana Stevan, Karen Dodd, Rae Knightly, and Sonia Garrett. You gave me the courage to go the "dark side," which looks pretty darn awesome to me! Thanks to early readers Deborah Kerbel, Helaine Becker, and Sandra Taylor, for your insights and invaluable feedback!
Finally thanks to my family for always being supportive. Love you all!

NEXT IN THE EERIE TALES FROM THE EAST SERIES

HAUNTED
The Cursed Lake

HAUNTED
THE CURSED LAKE
EERIE TALES FROM THE EAST
MAHTAB NARSIMHAN

CHAPTER 1

Jonah brought the axe down with such force that the block shattered. A large piece of wood splashed into the water, sending ripples toward the center of the lake. A patch the size of a rowboat, beyond the buoys, remained undisturbed. Oily calm.

Strange, thought Jonah, as he massaged his aching back. He shielded his eyes from the glare of the sun and stared at the spot for a while longer. If only he had time for a quick dip, he would have a chance to investigate. Was there a current in that section which kept the water so calm when the rest wasn't?

A gust of breeze wafted toward him, bringing a myriad of smells—water, sunshine, fresh grass, damp wood and an underlying tinge of something putrid. An animal had probably died in the forest on the far side of the lake. He'd have to ask Mom about it and get the caretaker, Frank, to find it and bury it. The smell would get worse as it got hotter.

Jonah stood at the edge of the water. The oily, calm patch had disappeared. A wind ruffled the surface of the lake, and the sun poked golden fingers into its sandy bottom, pockmarked with algae-covered rocks. How awesome would it be to swim and then lie on the grass with a book—

"Jonah! Stop dreaming and hurry. I need help with the cabins."

Summer had just begun, but Mom's voice was already tinged with exhaustion and impatience. This was their first year running Camp Sunny Acres since they'd bought it last fall. If they didn't do well this season, it was all over.

"Coming!" he called out.

As Jonah stacked the wood in the shelter beside the lake, he breathed in a lungful of resin and something earthy, like mushrooms. Birds squawked raucously overhead, playing tag. If only he could be a real camper and look forward to a summer filled with nothing but swimming, sports, crafts, and reading. But since Dad died two years ago, life had changed for the Anders family. His last summer had gone by in a whirl of bagging groceries and babysitting. They had needed the money. Running a camp this year had to be better.

Stay positive, he reminded himself. Dad would have wanted him to be brave and look after Mom. He was the man of the family now, and he had to stop feeling sorry for himself.

Mrs. Rastogi, the cook, whom they had inherited when they bought Sunny Acres, walked toward the cafeteria with an armload of groceries. Plump, with a kind laugh and salt-pepper hair, which she wore in a plait down to her waist, she was hands-down the best cook ever!

"Let me help," said Jonah as he hurried up to her.

"Thank you, Jonah," said Mrs. Rastogi, letting him take a few bags from her arms. "Ready for the campers? It's going to be nonstop for the next eight weeks."

"I know," said Jonah, trying not to sound mournful.

"What's the matter?" said Mrs. Rastogi.

Jonah shrugged as they trudged up the pathway between the cabins. The place looked rundown and in need of repairs and a fresh coat of paint, but he still loved it. Would the campers like it enough to come back next year? Could he and Mom make a success of Camp Sunny Acres, or would they have to pack up and leave in the winter? The questions wouldn't stop bugging him like a cloud of mosquitoes.

"There's so much to learn and do out here," said Jonah. "I hope we do it right! I love this place already and don't want to leave."

"None of us know what Fate has in store for us," said Mrs. Rastogi softly. "You come to me if you need any help or if something is bothering you. Okay?"

Jonah flicked a glance over his shoulder at the lake. The sun was high in the sky and its surface glittered with a million diamonds. A breeze cooled his warm face. Did he dare ask her about that weird patch in the water? Would she think it was his imagination and laugh at him?

"Sure," he said. "Thanks, Mrs. R."

They'd reached the cafeteria and entered through the back door into the kitchen. He placed the groceries carefully on the table.

"Anything else?" he asked her.

"Just this," said Mrs. Rastogi, taking an ice cream sandwich from the freezer. She handed it to Jonah. "Finish that *before* you meet the campers, or they'll all want one before lunch."

"Thanks," said Jonah.

He took the long way back to the camp office, strolling beside the lake as he bit into the cold sandwich, enjoying the sweetness on his tongue. There was a loud honk and the crunch of gravel. The busload of campers had arrived. They'd need help to register, find their cabins, and settle in. Then a tour of the camp, so they knew where everything was before heading for lunch. Better hurry. If Mom had to call out twice, there'd be fireworks before Canada Day.

As he turned away, a movement caught his eye. A wave tiptoed stealthily to shore. Jonah watched as it sidled up to the sandy bank and spent itself in a hiss of foam. His heartbeat quickened. There were no fish in this lake. No boat had gone by. So where did the wave come from?

Just as he turned and ran to the camp office, someone whispered his name so softly he wasn't sure if he'd heard or imagined it.

"Jonah."

To CONTINUE READING PLEASE FIND the book here: https://www.amazon.com/dp/B09QHCL97X

Made in the USA
Columbia, SC
02 May 2022